STACEY'S BROKEN HEART

**Other books by
Ann M. Martin**

Rachel Parker, Kindergarten Show-off
Eleven Kids, One Summer
Ma and Pa Dracula
Yours Turly, Shirley
Ten Kids, No Pets
Slam Book
Just a Summer Romance
Missing Since Monday
With You and Without You
Me and Katie (the Pest)
Stage Fright
Inside Out
Bummer Summer

BABY-SITTERS LITTLE SISTER series
THE BABY-SITTERS CLUB mysteries
THE BABY-SITTERS CLUB series

STACEY'S BROKEN HEART

Ann M. Martin

AN
APPLE
PAPERBACK

SCHOLASTIC INC.
New York Toronto London Auckland Sydney

The author gratefully acknowledges
Suzanne Weyn
for her help in
preparing this manuscript.

No part of this publication may be reproduced in whole or in part, or stored in a retrieval system, or transmitted in any form or by any means, electronic, mechanical, photocopying, recording, or otherwise, without written permission of the publisher. For information regarding permission, write to Scholastic Inc., 555 Broadway, New York, NY 10012.

ISBN 0-590-69205-4

12 11 10 9 8 7 6 5 4 3 2 1   6 7 8 9/9 0 1/0

Printed in the U.S.A.   40

First Scholastic printing, August 1996

STACEY'S BROKEN HEART

CHAPTER 1

Oh, no! I thought as a girl with dark brown hair and a wide smile walked toward us. *Things were going so well, too.* My perfect summer day with Robert was about to be ruined.

I reached over and took Robert's hand, intertwining my fingers with his. He'd just bitten into a tuna sandwich on a roll, but he smiled at me with his eyes. I returned his smile.

We had spent the whole morning together playing tennis. (He'd won three games and I'd won three.) Then we'd biked to the deli and brought back lunch, which we were now eating as we sat on a green bench by the outdoor courts. It was perfect end-of-summer weather, warm but with a cool breeze. The day had been so much fun. I wanted it to go on — undisturbed by Andi Gentile — forever.

Robert hadn't yet noticed Andi Gentile approaching. He was looking at me. Maybe if I pretended I didn't see her he wouldn't notice

1

her, either. Maybe she'd just keep walking.

I swiveled around and acted fascinated by a tennis game at one of the courts behind us. (And I do mean *acted*. The two people playing were moving at a snail's pace.) "Look, Robert," I said. "Doesn't that guy have a great serve?"

"I guess," Robert said, eyeing the game skeptically. "It's kind of slow motion."

"Hi, guys," Andi exclaimed.

No luck.

"Oh, hi, Andi," I replied with casual friendliness as I turned away from the slowest game of tennis on earth.

"Andi! Hi!" Robert said, quickly wiping at his mouth with a white deli napkin. He swallowed his tuna in one big gulp. "How are you?"

"Okay," she replied, rocking on the soles of her gleaming white sneakers and casually swinging her chrome tennis racket.

I didn't like the way he was smiling at Andi. *Calm down, Stacey*, I ordered myself. There was no reason to worry about Andi. Robert and Andi were just friends.

"I'm meeting Sheila here for tennis," Andi informed us as if that were great news.

Not Sheila MacGregor, too! I thought. Of all the girls who hang around with Robert's old crowd of friends, Andi and Sheila are not the worst. Not by far. I even sort of like Andi. But I wasn't in the mood to hang out with them today. I didn't want them spoiling this time with Robert.

You see, lately Robert has been spending less and less time with his old crowd and I want it to stay that way. Those kids have caused me so much grief, you wouldn't believe it. They almost got me in trouble for shoplifting, and I even stopped hanging around with my real friends because of them.

Sure, they're popular kids and all, but I think their values are the pits. *They're* not what I'd call true friends at all.

Believe me, I know what real friends are because I have them. Seven of them to be exact. Kristy, Mary Anne, Abby, Claudia (my very best friend), Mallory, Jessi, and Dawn. (Even though Dawn has moved to California, she's still a friend.) When you add me — Stacey McGill — we make up eight devoted friends who would do anything for one another. We're even in a club together, the Babysitters Club. I'll tell you more about that later.

For now, though, let me get back to the story of my ruined summer day. (Well, almost ruined, anyway.)

I definitely did *not* like the way Robert was smiling at Andi. Not that Robert isn't allowed to smile at other people. That would be ridiculous. But it was the *way* he was smiling that bothered me. He was smiling with his eyes and his mouth, smiling as though he were really glad to be talking to Andi.

Andi was telling Robert this supposedly funny story about how a friend of theirs, Jacqui Grant, got caught going from movie to movie at the quadraplex in the Washington Mall. I know it's not the worst crime on earth, but still, those kids are always doing things like that. They're always getting into trouble and they seem to think it's funny.

Apparently Andi thought this story about Jacqui was hysterical. She was nearly breathless with laughter. "And then . . . and then . . ." she gasped, struggling to speak through all her laughing. "When the usher wasn't looking, she ducked into the Disney movie and had to crawl down the aisle to get away from him."

Robert roared with laughter at this. "I can just picture her crawling around in the dark," he said.

"I know! I know!" Andi laughed, putting her hand on Robert's shoulder as if she were laughing so hard she needed him to hold her up. "Guess how she got caught? She got her foot stuck between two seats. When the usher came after her she was sprawled in the middle of the aisle. Helpless! She couldn't even move!

4

She just looked up at him and said, 'I seem to be stuck.' "

That really set them off. Even I had to smile, not because I thought it was so funny but because their laughter was contagious.

They were doubled over with hysterics, and I was so distracted by them that we didn't notice Sheila until she was right in front of us. While Andi was dressed in tennis whites, Sheila wore a tight purple unitard that showed off her perfect figure. (All Sheila's outfits show off her figure.) She tossed back her silky, thick blonde hair. "What's so funny?" she asked.

"I'm telling Robert and Stacey what happened to Jacqui," Andi replied, panting.

"Oh, isn't that hysterical?" Sheila laughed.

"Hey," Andi said. "Why don't we play doubles?"

"Yeah, why not?" Robert agreed, scooping his racket up off the bench.

"No thanks," I said, my voice overlapping Robert's. "We've already played six games. I'm pretty pooped."

"Oh, that's right," Sheila said with sickly sweet sympathy. "Your illness and all."

"No, it's not that," I said quickly. "I'm just tired." Sheila was referring to the fact that I'm diabetic, which means my body has trouble controlling the sugar levels in my bloodstream. Diabetes is a serious disease but I can live a normal life as long as I give myself injections of insulin every day and stick to a strict, healthy diet. (No sweets. Or my system would go wild and I could even go into a coma.) There's no doubt that having diabetes is a major drag, but I don't let it stop me from doing anything I want to do.

"I guess we won't play then," Robert said, looking disappointed.

"You can, if you want," I offered, knowing full well he wouldn't.

"Come on," Andi coaxed him. "One quick game."

"No, thanks. Another time," Robert said. Waving, Sheila and Andi went off to play their tennis game. Robert turned to me. "Do you feel all right? Do you want to go home?"

"I feel fine," I answered honestly. "I just didn't want to play tennis with them."

Robert nodded. He knows how I feel about his friends so I didn't have to explain. "Okay," he said. "What do you want to do now?"

"I don't know," I admitted with a shrug. "Want to try that new computer game my dad gave me? Mom and I set it up last night. It's pretty fun."

Robert stood up. "Sounds cool. But will your mother mind me being in the living room?" (Mom's rule is that Robert is allowed to come into the house while she's at work, but we have to stay in the kitchen. "The TV is definitely in your living room, remember?" he added.

Personally I didn't see any difference between being in the kitchen and being in the living room. "I'll call her when we get to my house. I'm sure she won't care as long as I let her know."

We took our bikes from the nearby bike rack and put our rackets into my basket. As we rode through Stoneybrook (our quiet Connecticut town) I thought about Andi and Sheila. Why had I let them bug me? Andi was really okay, and Sheila had been the one who first let me know that Robert liked me. They weren't horrible.

Was it because I felt that Robert wanted to hang out with them? Possibly. I wanted him to want to be with me — only me. Was that jealousy? Maybe.

I didn't want to be jealous. I don't think jealousy is a particularly attractive trait in a person. "We can go back and play tennis with them," I told Robert as we pulled up alongside each other at a stop sign.

"No, it's okay," Robert said. "It sounded like fun at the time, but I know you're not really wild about Andi and Sheila."

"They're all right, I suppose, but, you know . . . I want to spend the time with you," I explained.

"Yeah, me, too," Robert said. "I'd rather be with you, too."

We pushed off on our bikes and I suddenly felt light and happy. My perfect day with Robert hadn't been ruined after all. I was glad he'd rather be with me. My worries had been silly.

I promised myself never again to let mistrust or jealousy get the best of me. Robert and I were tight. Definitely. Nothing could change that.

When we reached my house, I used my keys to let us in the side door. Since it was Monday, Mom was still at work. The house was quiet. Which was why I jumped when the phone rang.

"Hello?" I said when I'd recovered from my surprise. It was Dad!

My mom and dad are divorced. My dad still lives in Manhattan, which is where I lived most of my life. I spend lots of weekends with him in the city, which I love. Not only do I get to see Dad, I get to spend time in Manhattan. I am a huge fan of New York City. (Not that I hate Stoneybrook or anything. I like it here, too. But this way I get the best of both worlds.)

"Hi, honey," Dad said. "I thought I'd just

call and say hello." We talked awhile about his work. (Dad's a workaholic.) I told him about playing tennis with Robert. He told me he'd gone Rollerblading in Central Park with his friend (girlfriend?) Samantha. We agreed to Rollerblade together the next Saturday when I came to visit.

I had just hung up when the phone rang again. "Sorry," I said to Robert, who'd sat down at the kitchen table and was reading *Time* magazine. "Whoever this is, I won't stay on long."

"Don't worry. It's cool," he said. "I'm reading this article on Michael Jordan."

I picked up the phone and was greeted by a female voice I recognized from somewhere. I just couldn't remember where. "Hello. Stacey?"

"Mrs. Walker!" I cried, suddenly remembering. "Hi! How are you?" Mr. and Mrs. Walker are a couple who live in our old Manhattan apartment building, the one we lived in before Mom and Dad split up. They have two adorable kids whom I'd baby-sat for a bunch of times. The Walkers are both artists. (She illustrates books and he does huge oil paintings.) Their apartment is crammed with great art.

"We're all fine," Mrs. Walker replied. "And I'm calling because Mr. Walker and I are wildly busy these days. We're trying to pull together a joint showing of our work at the Fitzroy Gallery."

"The Fitzroy is major!" I said. The Fitzroy is a big gallery several blocks away from where they live. Famous artists show their work there. It was a very big deal for the Walkers to have an exhibit there.

Mrs. Walker laughed lightly. "Yes, it is major. And we desperately want it to be perfect. Unfortunately the day camp Henry and Grace are now attending ends this Friday. Gabriel and I will never be ready for the show on time if we have the children underfoot all next week."

"So you need a baby-sitter," I guessed.

"Desperately!" she exclaimed. "We are madly in need of your services."

I chuckled to myself. I really like Mrs. Walker, but she has a funny, very melodramatic way of talking. Everything is desperate! Mad! Hopeless! Fabulous! To me, it makes her seem very artistic, very New York.

"Could you come and spend the week, Stacey?" she asked. "I was thinking you could stay with your father and then come baby-sit everyday. We would be forever grateful and, of course, we'd pay you."

A whole week in New York! "I'd love to!" I said, without even thinking. I'd be with Dad.

I'd be in the city. And, I'd be with the Walkers.

The Walkers know tons of interesting, sometimes even famous, people. Their place is always full of excitement. Grace and Henry are cute, too. What could be better?

"I'll have to check with Mom and Dad," I added. "But I think it will be fine. I don't see why not."

Mrs. Walker sighed deeply. "I hope so. I can't tell you what a relief this is. Thank you! Thank you! Thank you!"

"You're welcome. When do you need me to start?"

"Could you be here this coming Saturday?"

"I think so. I was coming in to visit Dad, anyway."

"Super! Just super! Call me tonight to let me know for sure."

"All right," I agreed. "I hope I'll see you next Saturday."

"Wow! You look happy," Robert said as I hung up. "What was that about?"

I told him, and his face fell. "A whole week!" he exclaimed.

"It's just one week," I said.

"But it's the end of the summer," he protested. "We won't have much more free time before school."

"Aw, come on, Robert," I said, sitting beside him at the table. "It's not like we won't see each other once school starts. We'll see each other every day in school. The week will go really fast. This is a chance for me to make some money and see my father. The Walkers are cool people, too."

"Well, I suppose," Robert said in a slightly sulky voice. "I'll miss you, though."

His words made me happy. I was glad he'd miss me. "I'll miss you, too," I said, laying my hand on his wrist. "But the time will go by like nothing. You'll see."

"I hope so," he mumbled, forcing a smile.

"It will," I insisted. "A week is nothing."

I didn't know then that the week wasn't going to be nothing. It turned out to be really something.

CHAPTER 2

Robert and I started to play the computer game my dad gave me, *Marvel in the Mist*. (I had phoned Mom and she said it was okay for us to stay in the living room together.) We played for three and a half hours. We might have played longer but I had to leave for my BSC meeting.

BSC is short for Baby-sitters Club — it's what almost everyone calls the club. At 5:20 I arrived at my friend Claudia's house on Bradford Court, which is where our meetings are always held. I knew it was 5:20 exactly because I checked Claudia's digital clock as soon as I stepped into her bedroom. Kristy, our president, is a real nut about being on time.

"Hi, Stacey," Claudia greeted me.

"Hey, look at you!" Abby said, smiling. She sat cross-legged on Claudia's bed. "Where did you get the Florida tan? Did you use that instant tan stuff that comes in a tube?"

"Oh, no way!" Kristy laughed and grimaced at the same time. She sat in her usual spot, Claudia's director's chair. "That stuff's too weird. You didn't use that, did you, Stacey?"

"Tennis," I told them. "I guess I got tan playing tennis. But what's wrong with that tanning stuff? I think it's kind of cool." Kristy, Abby, Claudia, and I started discussing artificial tanning creams while we waited for the others to arrive.

As we talked, I checked out my image in the mirror. Even though I wore sunblock, I *was* tan. Cool. I know it's not supposed to be great for your skin, but my eyes always look bluer when I'm tan. I quickly picked out my blonde shoulder-length perm with my fingers and turned back to the conversation.

"I get tan even though I wear sunblock," Abby complained.

"You're lucky," said Kristy.

As this talk went on I started to think how lucky I was to have good friends like my BSC pals. Even when we have light conversations like this, I feel so warm and at ease. Totally accepted. My BSC friends know me well and like me as I am. It's a great feeling.

But before I go any further, let me tell you about the BSC and its members. First, a crash course in BSC history. Ready?

It all started with Kristy Thomas's great idea.

The idea was: have a single phone number where parents can contact several qualified baby-sitters at once. This saves parents from having to call all around town looking for a sitter. Simple, but brilliant. Most of Kristy's many ideas are like that.

In the beginning, the several qualified baby-sitters were Kristy (of course), her best friend Mary Anne, their good friend Claudia, and me. I'd just moved to Stoneybrook and become friends with Claudia. She was the one who suggested me for the club. We put up fliers advertising the club, listing Claudia's phone number since she has her own private line. Then we sat in her room and waited.

We didn't wait long. The phone started ringing almost immediately. In no time, we were so busy that we invited Dawn — who had moved from California to Stoneybrook — to join. Things were going great.

Then, disaster struck.

Not disaster, really. But it felt like it at the time. Dad's company transferred him back to Manhattan, so my family had to pack up and leave. The BSC was then short one member, but had more clients than ever. That was when Mallory and Jessi came on as junior BSC officers. They're junior because they're younger (eleven) than the rest of us, who are thirteen.

Things during my short stay in Manhattan

were interesting, to say the least. The bad news was that Mom and Dad split up. The good news was that I returned to Stoneybrook with Mom. It *was* good, too, because although I'm wild for Manhattan, I missed my Stoneybrook friends terribly. I was glad to be back and they were happy to have me. Club business was booming and they needed me badly.

Not long afterward, I left the club for awhile. That's because I got the crazy idea that the girls in Robert's group were cooler than my BSC friends. What a laugh! When I think that I almost lost my true friends because of those girls, it gives me the chills. Once I saw how wrong I'd been I rejoined the club. Kristy let me come back on probation (which meant I was on trial), but now I'm as in as ever before.

After I rejoined the BSC, Dawn moved to California permanently. (She missed it too much.) We have a new member now, Abby. She's Dawn's replacement (not that anyone could *replace* Dawn, but you know what I mean).

Now that you know our history, here's how the club works. We meet every Monday, Wednesday, and Friday from five-thirty until six. Clients call during that time. The person nearest the phone answers and takes down the client's information (name, number, how

16

many kids, when, where). We decide who should take the job and then call the client back.

It sounds simple, and it is, but it takes a lot of planning and organization to keep everything running smoothly. That's the reason we each have official club titles and responsibilities to go along with those titles.

As you know, Kristy Thomas is president. This is partly because she thought of the club and partly because the club needs someone strong, organized, and . . . well, bosslike to keep it going. (Is bosslike the same as bossy? I think so.) Kristy is all those things and is very dedicated to the club. On top of that she constantly overflows with great ideas.

One of her ideas was to keep a club notebook, a journal in which we write about our sitting jobs. It's a great reference when you need to know about a certain family you'll be baby-sitting for.

Her other very important idea was the record book. That's where we keep the schedule of who is baby-sitting where and when. We also have our personal schedules in there. For example, the book says when I'll be in Manhattan with Dad, when I have a doctor's appointment, and so on. That way if I'm not available to work on a certain day, it's in the book. In the back of the book is official information about our clients: addresses, phone numbers, the rates they pay. There's even special information about our charges such as allergies or their likes and dislikes.

Also under the category of great Kristy ideas come Kid-Kits. These are boxes full of fun stuff to bring on baby-sitting jobs. Each of us has our own and we keep them stocked with things such as stickers, coloring books, arts and crafts materials, and games. Kids love the Kid-Kits, though we don't bring them all the time. We tend to use them to smooth the way in difficult sitting jobs. We use our club dues to refill the boxes once in awhile.

Speaking of dues, I'm the club treasurer. I got that job because I love math and I'm good at it. I have the sometimes unpleasant duty of collecting dues every week. Everyone grumbles on dues day, but it's necessary. We use the money to contribute to Claudia's phone bill. We also pay Kristy's brother Charlie to drive Kristy and Abby across town since they live farther away than the rest of us. If there's anything left over, we restock Kid-Kits or buy anything else we might need. Then, if we have enough money (as treasurer, I decide this) we can do something fun such as go to the movies or have a pizza party.

Our vice-president is Claudia. Her main contribution is the use of her phone and her room. She's also a kind of hospitality officer, providing snacks and soda for everyone. She always makes sure there's a healthy snack for me, which I appreciate a lot.

Mary Anne is our secretary. After Kristy, she has the second most important job (in my opinion). She keeps track of the record book, seeing who is available for jobs and then recording the jobs in the book. She's unbelievably good at it, and has never made a mistake.

We also have an alternate officer. That's the person who has to know everyone's club job and be ready to take over if someone is not at a meeting. Before she left, Dawn was the alternate. Now Abby is.

As I mentioned before, Jessi and Mallory are our junior officers. They're only allowed to baby-sit during the day (or in the evenings for their own families). That frees the rest of us to take night jobs, so they're a big help.

Now I'll tell you a bit about the members of our club. Again, I'll start with Kristy. Once Dad and I went to see a play called *The Mouse That Roared*. The title always makes me think of Kristy. At first glance she looks a little mousy — petite with straight brown hair, plain, sporty clothes, no makeup. But she sure can roar. She lets you know exactly what she's thinking. She's not at all shy about it even if her opinion is unpopular or a little insulting.

This domineering personality allows her to take charge of things easily. She really keeps the club moving. (No one goofs off or breaks rules with Kristy around.) She also coaches a little kids' softball team called Kristy's Krushers, which gives her plenty of roaring opportunities.

Don't get me wrong, though. Kristy isn't just bossy. She's also a good friend with a great sense of humor. But she has a very can-do attitude.

Kristy has needed that attitude. Her life has not always been easy. Her family used to live on Bradford Court across the street from Claudia and next door to Mary Anne. Mrs. Thomas struggled to raise four kids (Kristy has two older brothers and one younger) by herself since Kristy's dad walked out on them right after her younger brother, David Michael, was born. (Is that rotten, or what?) Then, the most amazing thing happened. Kristy's mom met this man named Watson Brewer and remarried. The amazing part is that Watson is an actual millionaire, complete with a mansion and everything! Kristy and her family moved across town to live in the mansion.

Her family needs a mansion, too. Kristy's mom and Watson adopted a Vietnamese girl, Emily Michelle, who is two and a half. Nannie, Kristy's cool, peppy grandmother, came to help take care of Emily. On top of that, Watson is divorced and he has two kids, Karen (seven) and Andrew (four). They live with Kristy and her family every other month, and with their mother and her new husband the rest of the time. With their assorted pets, that's a full house.

Despite living in a mansion and being suddenly wealthy, Kristy wasn't thrilled with the move. (Material things don't mean much to her.) She didn't like being so far away from the rest of us. And she wasn't sure if she liked Watson, either. But soon everything straightened out. Watson turned out to be a terrific guy, and Kristy is wild about her new stepsiblings. (They adore her, too.)

One person who really missed Kristy when she moved across town was Mary Anne Spier. She and Kristy had always lived next door to each other and they were almost like sisters — twins, even, since they looked a lot alike back then. Mary Anne is also petite with brown hair. But, unlike Kristy, she's softspoken, even a bit shy.

Of course, Mary Anne and Kristy stayed friends even though they couldn't talk to each other from their bedroom windows anymore. When I think of how Mary Anne was when I first met her, it's amazing how much she's changed. She was this timid little kid with braids who wore awful, babyish outfits (pleated skirts, ruffled blouses, knee socks). Since she was short, too, she seemed much younger than she was. She dressed like that because her father was very strict. Her mother died when Mary Anne was a baby and Mr. Spier had to raise Mary Anne by himself. He did a good job, *too* good. He sort of overdid it, if you ask me. He watched her *so* carefully and had so many rules that Mary Anne could make few choices for herself, including what she'd wear and how she'd fix her hair.

Now Mary Anne looks her age, wears a little makeup, has adorable short blunt cut hair and is, in fact, extremely cute. She won the freedom to develop a new image thanks to Dawn Schafer and her mom. They loosened Mr. Spier up a lot (thank goodness!). He relaxed enough to let Mary Anne be herself.

I should explain. See, Dawn's mother married Mary Anne's father. Dawn's parents had gotten divorced, which was why Dawn had moved to Stoneybrook with her mother and her younger brother, Jeff. (Her dad stayed in Palo City, California.) When Dawn and Mary Anne browsed through Mrs. Schafer's old high school yearbook they made an awesome discovery: Their parents had been boyfriend and girlfriend back then. Right away, they started scheming to get their parents back together.

It worked, too! Although not overnight. It took months, actually. But finally their parents married. Mary Anne and her father left Bradford Court and went to live in Dawn's old farmhouse (built in 1795!). The four of them (Jeff had returned to California) had to work hard to become a new family. It wasn't nearly as easy as Mary Anne and Dawn had expected. They even had some upsetting fights along the way.

One of their main problems was food. Dawn and her mother are health food eaters. (They don't touch red meat, sugar, or junk food, and actually prefer foods like tofu, miso, and kelp flakes.) Mary Anne and her dad eat red meat, fried foods, and lots of other things people who are health conscious *don't* eat. Mealtimes turned into battles. There were other problems, such as messiness versus neatness. (Dawn's mother is messy; Mary Anne's father is neat.) There were the issues of privacy and space. (Mary Anne and Dawn started out sharing a room and ended up much happier with separate ones.) Eventually, though, everyone compromised a little and things worked out.

That is, they worked out until Dawn began missing California. She missed her father, her brother Jeff, her friends, and her life there in general. I think she tried not to miss it because she was loyal to her friends here, Mary Anne in particular. But that longing got the best of her and she decided to live in California permanently. Mary Anne was heartbroken at first, but now she's used to the idea.

It helps that her boyfriend, Logan Bruno, is such a nice guy. He and Mary Anne are very close and being with him helps her feel less alone now that Dawn is gone. Logan is an associate member of the BSC. That means we call him if we have a job that no one else can take. He's a good baby-sitter since he has a younger brother and sister of his own.

Not only does Mary Anne have Logan to depend on, she has us, too — the BSC. We all care about Mary Anne. She's an amazing club secretary, a sensitive listener, and a true friend.

Speaking of true friends, my very closest friend is Claudia Kishi. She was the first one to befriend me when I moved here and we've been best friends ever since. Claudia and I have a lot in common. For one thing, we both love clothing and style. Claudia's style is much more original than mine, though. Her creative, great-looking outfits reflect the fact that Claudia is an artist. Everything about her is artistic. She loves to draw, paint, sculpt, make jewelry, throw pottery, silk-screen — everything!

Today Claudia had on an oversized purple top over turquoise leggings. With fabric paints she'd painted a beautiful unicorn on the top and then decorated the leggings with designs in the same colors. From her ears dangled earrings she'd made of papier-mâché in the shape of unicorn heads.

One thing Claudia and I *don't* have in common is junk food. I can't have any and Claudia is wild for it. Her parents don't approve so Claudia stashes it all over her room. You have to be careful when you sit down somewhere or you just might squash a pack of Devil Dogs or crush a bag of chips.

Another thing you might find hidden in Claudia's bedroom are her Nancy Drew mysteries. Claudia absolutely devours them, but her parents don't think they're intellectual enough. That seems crazy to me, but if you think about Claudia's family, it makes sense. Mrs. Kishi is the head librarian at the Stoneybrook library so I suppose her taste in books is pretty sophisticated. And Claudia's older sister Janine (who's sixteen) is a real live genius with an IQ score to prove it.

It's funny to think that two sisters could be as different as Claudia and Janine. Claudia's style is funky and artistic, while Janine has *no* style.

Another difference. Claudia is gorgeous, Janine isn't. Claudia has astounding, thick, silky black hair and almond-shaped eyes. (The

Kishis are Japanese-American.) She's glamourous and graceful. Janine, on the other hand, is very plain and couldn't care less about her looks. Claudia once gave her a makeover, though, and it's helped some.

And while Janine adores nothing more than sitting in front of her computer, Claudia can hardly stand school. Schoolwork doesn't come easily to her and her spelling is the pits. (If you saw the club notebook, you'd see what I mean.) I believe Claudia isn't good at schoolwork because she can't bring herself to pay attention. She's always concocting some new art project in her head instead of listening to the teacher. Then when she's home, instead of studying, she's working on that project.

Speaking of sisters who are different, our newest member, Abby, has a sister, Anna, who looks exactly like her. They're twins. They both have very dark eyes and wear either contacts or glasses. They have thick, curly brown hair, but they each wear it differently; Abby's is long and Anna's is short.

Honestly, though, apart from their looks, Abby and Anna Stevenson are almost as different as Claudia and Janine. Anna is a musician devoted to playing the violin. Abby is an athlete who loves to play soccer and helps Kristy with the Krushers. (She lives two doors down from Kristy on McLelland Road, so it's convenient for them to go to games and practices together.) Even though Abby suffers from occasional asthma attacks and has lots of allergies, she doesn't let it slow her down.

The Stevensons are originally from Long Island, which isn't far from Manhattan. Their father died in a car accident when Anna and Abby were nine. Their mother works as an editor and commutes to and from the city every day. She works hard and sometimes gets home late, so Anna and Abby have become very self-sufficient and independent.

When Dawn moved back to California, we invited both Anna and Abby to join the BSC. Anna didn't want to take the time away from her violin practice, but Abby said yes. It's funny to see how Abby interacts with Kristy. They're so different, yet both are outspoken and take-charge types. I think Abby is having trouble taking orders from Kristy even though she likes her a lot.

Shannon Kilbourne also lives on McLelland Road along with Kristy, Abby, and Anna. In fact, she's good friends with Anna. Shannon is another associate club member, like Logan. For awhile she was coming to meetings and we thought she could take over for Dawn. But Shannon's very active in after-school activities and she simply didn't have the time. She still comes to meetings once in awhile when she's free and can get a ride to Claudia's with Kristy and Abby.

That covers the thirteen-year-olds, but I could never leave out our junior officers, Jessi and Mallory. They're best friends, too.

Jessi Ramsey is a talented ballerina who takes classes in Stamford (the city closest to Stoneybrook). She looks like a ballerina, with long legs and graceful arms. Her black hair is usually pulled back in a bun or a braid the way dancers wear it. She has a pretty face and smooth, dark skin.

Jessi lives in the house my family moved out of when my dad was transferred back to New York. She and her family (which consists of her mom, dad, younger sister Becca, baby brother Squirt, and her Aunt Cecelia) had come to Stoneybrook because her father's company transferred him to their Stamford office. The fact that the Ramseys are African-American bent some of their neighbors out of shape for awhile. This was a shock to Jessi because her old neighborhood had been well integrated. But before long, the jerky neighbors chilled out and the Ramseys made some good friends.

Mallory Pike is also talented, like Jessi, although she isn't a dancer. Mallory wants to be a writer-illustrator of children's books when she gets older. She'll have lots of kids to test her stories on since she has seven younger brothers and sisters. After Mal, there are the triplets, Byron, Jordan, and Adam (who are ten years old), Vanessa (nine), Nicky (eight), Margo (seven), and Claire (five).

Somehow I know Mallory will be successful as a writer-illustrator. She has a funny, original way of looking at things. She says she loathes the idea of having her author picture on the back of a book or on the jacket flap. That's because she doesn't like her looks very much. She has curly reddish-brown hair, glasses, braces, freckles, and a great smile. Okay, so it's not the standard beautiful-girl look, but Mal has an inner beauty and I think she really shines.

So that's our crew. By five-thirty we were assembled and ready to begin the meeting. "Any new business?" Kristy asked from the director's chair.

"I won't be here for a week," I announced. As I told them about the Walker job I could see Kristy's expression growing grimmer and grimmer. "What's wrong?" I asked.

"You keep doing this!" she exploded, tossing her arms up in the air, which caused her baseball cap to tumble backward off her head.

"Doing what?" I demanded indignantly.

"Taking long-term jobs. You took that every-day job at the Cheplins'. And now this!"

Awhile back I'd sat for two kids every day after school until it got to be too much. Kristy hadn't wanted me to take the job because it left the club minus one sitter.

"Kristy," I said, "what is the difference if I take a different baby-sitting job every day of the week or baby-sit for the same people all week?"

"I understand what you're saying," she said, picking up her cap. "But you take these jobs with people we don't usually work for. Our regular customers depend on us to have enough sitters to cover them."

"It's just for one week," I protested.

"The worst possible week," Kristy grumbled. "I'll be away the same time. With you gone, Stacey, we'll be two members short."

"Late August is usually our slowest time," Mary Anne pointed out as she sat at the edge of the bed with the record book open on her lap. "So many of our clients are away on vacation."

A piece of Kristy's hair had fallen into her face. She blew it away and sighed. "I suppose. I don't feel good about it, though. I'm afraid things are going to get out of hand. Mary Anne, you're organized, why don't you take over as president while I'm gone?"

"Hey, wait!" Abby objected, rising to her knees from the spot on the floor where she was sitting. "Isn't that supposed to be my job? I'm alternate officer, aren't I?"

"Well, yeah," Kristy admitted. "Sure. But you just joined the club. And this isn't a regular job. This is president."

"President is a job just like any other job," Abby insisted.

"If you're president, then who will be treasurer while Stacey is gone?" Kristy countered. "You can't be president because you have to be treasurer."

"I'll do both," Abby said. "What's the big deal? I'll collect the dues. Stacey will be back in time to pay the bills and all the rest she does. Most of the time the alternate doesn't do anything. It's driving me crazy. I want to do something."

"Claudia is vice-president," Kristy said. "Maybe she should take over. That's what happens in the White House, the vice-president takes over if the president can't do it."

"They don't have an extremely bored alternate officer in the White House," Abby argued. "Besides, I hate to break it to you, but this *isn't* the White House."

Kristy glared at Abby a moment, then her expression softened. She rubbed the back of her neck thoughtfully. "All right," she said, leaning forward in the chair. "All right. You can take over as president *and* as treasurer."

Abby punched the air triumphantly. "Yes!"

"On one condition," Kristy put in quickly.

Abby's smile faded.

"The condition is that you run Wednesday's meeting. I'll be here and I'll decide if it goes well."

"How about if everyone decides," Abby countered shrewdly. "We'll vote at the end of the meeting. That's the only fair way."

"Okay," Kristy agreed, accepting the challenge. "It's a deal."

CHAPTER 3

The moment I woke up on Tuesday morning, I started thinking about what to pack for my week in the city. Somehow, when I'm in Manhattan, clothing seems more important to me than it does in Stoneybrook. I suppose that's because New York City is a fashion capital, and when you walk down the street you see so many great styles. Of course, not *everyone* in the city dresses great, but there are more stores than in Stoneybrook and with much trendier clothes. And, in the suburbs, people dress in a more sporty, casual way than in the city.

Maybe I just didn't want to look like I was from the suburbs when I was in the city. I think that was it, really. After all, I am a city person, part-time, anyway.

I threw off my sheet and headed straight for my closet to pull out my suitcase. Normally, I don't pack a whole suitcase when I visit Dad for a weekend. My overnight bag is sufficient. But I would be gone for an entire week this time.

I dragged the suitcase out and tossed it onto my bed. Then I went back to my closet and began studying my clothes. Somehow, nothing there looked right to me.

I was so intent on staring into my closet that I didn't even hear Mom come in. "Going somewhere?" she asked.

I jumped back. "Oh, wow, Mom! You startled me."

"Sorry," she said with a smile. She looked nice, as she usually does. She was dressed in beige pants with a matching sleeveless tunic top, and had draped a long scarf around her neck. Her blonde hair was set in soft curls. I think Mom is pretty and, when people tell me I look like her, I'm glad.

"I don't have anything to take to the Walkers'," I complained.

"Nothing to take?" Mom laughed incredulously. "That closet is jammed full of clothes."

"I know," I admitted with a sigh. "Maybe my taste has changed or something."

"Well, we're due for a back-to-school shopping trip soon," Mom said. "We can do it before you go."

"Thank you!" I cried, hugging her. End of

summer is such a strange time in terms of clothing. All the fall school stuff is in the stores, but it's not cold enough yet to wear the things you buy. So, you get something new and you're excited to wear it, but then you roast. Most of the time I don't care. I wear it anyway and pretend (even to myself) that I'm not really hot.

"When can we go?" I asked.

"How about tomorrow?" Mom suggested. "It's a special employees-only back-to-school sale day. You can meet me at Bellair's after your BSC meeting."

"Great," I agreed.

Mom kissed my forehead. "Speaking of Bellair's, I'd better leave now or I'll be late for work. What are you doing today?"

I shrugged. "No plans. I'll call Robert or Claudia, I guess. I'll see what they're doing."

"Well, have a good day," Mom said as she left the room.

I changed from my white cotton nightgown into a pair of khaki-green Bermuda shorts and a yellow cotton shirt with purple violets on it. Heading downstairs, I decided to phone Robert first, since he'd made such a fuss about my going away for a week.

When I called his house, his younger sister answered. "He went out," she told me.

"Did he say where?" I asked, surprised. Robert hadn't mentioned any plans to me. He usually tells me if he's going somewhere the next day.

"No . . . oh, wait a minute, there's a note here in Robert's horrible handwriting." (Horrible? I like Robert's handwriting.) "It says, 'Tell Stacey I went to play basketball with some guys. I'll be gone all day.' That's where he is, I suppose."

"Okay, thanks a lot," I told her, hanging up. That made sense. Robert's guy friends never make plans. They always just do things on the spur of the moment.

Next, I phoned Claudia. "I'm in the middle of trying to make watermelon carvings," she said. "The watermelons were really cheap at the supermarket and they're an intense green color this time of year. You can come over and watch if you want. You could eat the watermelon insides. I'm not really using the melon part."

Somehow eating globs of mushy pink, pitty melon as Claudia carelessly tossed it out of its rind didn't sound appealing. Besides, when Claudia is deep in the throes of creativity, she's not great company. She's in her own world at those times. You talk to her and she nods, but you get the distinct feeling she hasn't heard anything you've said.

"No thanks," I said. "Call me later when you're done."

"Okay," Claud agreed, sounding relieved that I wasn't coming.

That left me with nothing to do, so I went back upstairs and packed the few items I knew I wanted to take with me. I selected my best earrings. I sorted through my sandals, sneakers, and dress shoes and decided I definitely needed a heavy-soled sandal for walking in the city.

As I packed, my mind wandered and I noticed something about myself. I wasn't at all upset about leaving Robert for the week. Why not? I wondered. I'm crazy about Robert. Shouldn't I miss him?

I'd be gone only a week, of course. No biggie. Still . . . was I heartless or something?

That idea stopped me cold. Heartless? Me? Was it possible?

No, of course not. The thought made me uncomfortable, just the same. And I was suddenly struck with an overwhelming need to see Robert — to feel again the excitement and happiness I feel whenever we're together.

Tossing a sock into my suitcase, I left my room and went downstairs. Robert and his friends always play basketball at the outdoor courts by our school. I decided to go and watch them. At least I'd get to see him and talk to him a little. Besides, he'd appreciate that I came out to see him. It would let him know that I cared about spending time with him. I wasn't just heartlessly going off for a week without thinking of him at all.

It isn't far from my house to SMS (Stoneybrook Middle School, where my friends and I attend school). When I arrived at the courts, sure enough a bunch of guys were playing basketball.

Right away, I recognized two of Robert's friends, a nice guy named Alex Zacharias and another named Wayne McConville. Some of the other guys I recognized from school but didn't really know. But I didn't see Robert.

Alex noticed me and waved. "Where's Robert?" he called to me.

"Isn't he here?" I shouted back.

Alex shook his head. "I called him to come and play but he said he had plans. I figured he was with you."

"No. If you see him, tell him I'm looking for him. Okay?"

"Okay," Alex agreed just as someone passed him the ball. Then he was off, dribbling down to the far end of the court.

I was stunned. I now knew two things. Robert was not playing basketball, as he'd said.

And he had plans — but not with me, obviously.

What did this mean?

I had no idea. But I didn't have a good feeling about it.

CHAPTER 4

On Wednesday, Abby entered Claudia's bedroom looking prepared to take over the meeting. Chin up, shoulders thrown back, she smiled confidently as she threw herself into the director's chair. "Hi, guys," she greeted Claudia and me.

Kristy, who walked in right behind her, scowled deeply when she saw that her chair was occupied. Abby didn't notice, or pretended not to. Claudia and I could only shrug helplessly at Kristy as she found a spot for herself on the bed.

Mary Anne came in next. Mary Anne did a double-take, looking at Abby casually, looking away, and then swinging back around, her brown eyes wide. We all laughed, except Kristy. "Oh," Mary Anne gasped. "I expected to see Kristy there."

"I'm in the president's chair today," Abby

said enthusiastically. I stole a peek at Kristy from the corner of my eye. Her lips were pressed together tightly and she looked pretty unhappy.

As the other members drifted in, my mind wandered. I started worrying about Robert again. He hadn't called me at all yesterday. This morning, I called him. And now I wasn't sure I believed what he'd had to say about where he was yesterday. He said he'd gone to the Stoneybrook Community Center courts to play one-on-one with Marty Bukowski. "I couldn't pass up a chance to play with the Bukeman," Robert said. "The Bukeman" is what they call Marty, who is the star basketball player at SMS.

"Why didn't you use the school courts, like always?" I asked.

"The Bukeman wanted to use the community center courts."

I was suspicious for two reasons. One, his note had said he would be playing with some guys, plural, more than one guy. And second, Robert doesn't usually hang out with Marty Bukowski. They know one another, but they're not good friends.

Other than that, the explanation made sense. Maybe I was being too suspicious.

By 5:29 everyone had arrived but Jessi and

Mallory. "I'm here! I'm here!" Jessi cried as she slid into the room like a baseball player sliding into home plate.

Abby leaned over the side of her chair and caught Jessi in a withering glare. Not only were her eyes narrowed, but her lip was lifted in a sneer. Jessi swallowed hard and cringed. "I'm giving you the Look," Abby said in a spooky voice. Curling her fingers into witch-like claws, she stretched them toward Jessi. "This look will frighten you so badly you will never be late for this or anything else again as long as you live!"

Jessi began to suspect that Abby was goofing on Kristy. She was still wary, though. "I'm not really late," she said, nodding toward the digital clock.

Abby relaxed her creepy posture and smiled. "In that case, forget it. I just thought I was supposed to give you that look from the crypt to scare you when you're late. I thought it was part of the job description."

"Not funny," I heard Kristy mumble under her breath as she folded her arms tightly.

"I was with Mallory," Jessi explained. "We were walking Pow." Pow is the Pikes' basset hound. "We didn't realize how late it was, but when we did, I ran straight here. Mal had to bring Pow home, but she's on her way."

As Jessi spoke, Mallory came racing into the

room. Immediately she checked the clock. It read 5:32. "Sorry! Sorry!" Mallory apologized to Kristy.

Kristy opened her mouth to say something, but Abby cut her off. "No problem, Mallory. This is your lucky day because I'm the president today and I'm not a maniac about punctuality. Two, three minutes, give or take, is cool with me."

Mallory smiled and sighed with relief as she sat on the floor beside Jessi. "Whew! Great!"

From the frown on her face, I suspected Kristy was just dying to say something to Mallory about her lateness, but she kept her downturned lips squeezed together and silently fumed.

"All right, we're all here." Abby began the meeting. "Any new business?"

"Good. I have some," she continued without a pause. "As you all know, today you are going to vote on whether or not you think I would make a good fill-in president while Kristy is vacationing in sunny Hawaii. So, I'd like to tell you some of the things you could expect with me as president."

"We won't have to be super on-time?" Mallory guessed.

"Right," said Abby. "You can't stroll in fifteen minutes late, but a minute or two or even five isn't a tragedy. Also, you won't have to write in the club notebook unless you have something important to say or unless you just feel like it."

"Great," Claudia said quietly. She hates writing in the club notebook.

"What?" Kristy yelped indignantly.

"I'm sorry, but I don't see the point of being forced to write when you don't have anything particularly interesting to say," Abby explained, defending her position. "Having to write about every single job, no matter how dull it was, is a waste of time in my opinion."

"If everyone just wrote when they felt like it, nothing would get written at all," Kristy objected.

"I'd write," Mallory said.

"That's because you like to write," Kristy shot back. "Not everyone does."

"Isn't this supposed to be fun?" Abby said. "Shouldn't we be allowed to do the things we *like*?"

"It's fun, but it's also a business," Kristy said hotly.

"I think we can run smoothly and still have fun," Abby said calmly. She straightened in the chair, facing forward. "Another change I intend to make is I'll cut dues to every other week rather than every week."

This announcement was met with a round of cheering.

"You can't do that!" Kristy cried.

"If I'm president I can," Abby replied. "And think about this. With less notebook writing, we'll need fewer notebooks. And, as long as you're away, we won't have to pay Charlie to drive you. I'll ride my bike here. I'm streamlining the organization, cutting the budget, and eliminating unnecessary paperwork. It's the way business is run today. My mother told me that's what they're doing in her publishing company."

For maybe the first time ever, Kristy was speechless. Amazing! Abby had out-talked her.

Abby addressed the rest of us. "No dues. It will certainly make my job as alternate treasurer a lot easier."

I wasn't sure how I felt about this. The treasury wouldn't miss the dues — much. And I wouldn't be here for most of Abby's short presidency, anyway.

But there was something about Abby's campaign speech that was unsettling. It didn't sound like she was campaigning for just one week. A person who was just filling in didn't propose sweeping changes. Yet the things she said made sense to me. We'd gotten so used to Kristy's strict rules that we took them for granted. But perhaps there was an easier way, a less rigid approach to conducting business.

From the pleased looks on everyone else's face (except Kristy's), it seemed to make sense to them, too.

"And another thing," Abby went on, but the ringing phone cut her off.

I was closest to the phone, so I scooped it up. "Hello. Baby-sitters Club," I said.

"Is Stacey there?" asked a familiar voice I couldn't place. It was a girl's voice. Definitely not a client.

"This is she," I said cautiously. Only clients usually call during this time.

"Hi, it's Emily Bernstein," the caller said. Now I knew her voice. Emily is a student at SMS whom most of us are friendly with. She's the editor of the school paper and very nice. "I'm sorry to call you here. I know it's club time. But I didn't have your home phone number and I really need to talk to you."

"That's all right, but I can't stay on long," I told her. "Just a sec." Everyone was staring at me for an explanation. I cupped the phone. "Emily Bernstein," I whispered.

"Make it quick," Kristy said. "You're tying up the phone."

"What's up, Emily?" I asked.

For a moment, she didn't reply. I thought maybe she'd put the phone down and walked away. Then she spoke in a nervous, uncertain voice. "I don't know if I should even be telling you this. I mean, I really almost didn't call. But then I thought I should. You really should know. If a person doesn't have the whole story she can't make a good decision."

Kristy began making circles in the air with her hands, signaling me to wrap it up.

"Just tell me, Emily, please," I prompted, not sure I really wanted to hear what she had to say. Her nervousness was making me nervous.

"It's about Robert," Emily began. "Yesterday I was at the mall and I saw him with another girl."

My heart banged into my chest, hard.

"What girl?" I asked, wishing everyone weren't looking at me.

"I wasn't sure. I only saw her from the back. She had dark hair. Robert turned around, though, and I know it was him. They were having lunch at Casa Grande at the Washington Mall. My mother and I were shopping for school clothes and we went to Casa Grande for lunch."

"Th-thanks for telling me," I managed to say, despite the fact that I was totally shocked.

"Okay. Are you all right?" Emily asked.

"Fine," I lied.

"I hope I did the right thing," Emily said.

"You did. Thanks. 'Bye." I hung up and I must have looked pretty dazed.

47

"What's the matter?" Claudia asked. "What was that all about?"

Slowly, I told them what Emily had told me. "Robert with another girl?" Kristy scoffed. "I don't believe it!"

"She saw them," I told her. "And Robert told me he was playing basketball with Marty Bukowski yesterday. He definitely lied to me."

"It could just be a misunderstanding," Mary Anne said. "Remember when the kids thought Logan was going out with Kristy? And all the while Kristy was only helping Logan pick out a Valentine's Day present for me."

"Yeah, or maybe Robert had to talk to a friend who really needed him but he didn't think you'd understand, so he lied," Claudia suggested.

Those possibilities made me feel a little better. But not a whole lot better. Something was up with Robert. I had to find out what.

During the rest of the meeting, my mind reeled with possibilities. Was Robert dating someone else? Was this a one-time thing, or was he about to dump me?

The phone rang several times but I didn't pay attention since I wouldn't be around to take new jobs. Who was this girl? Was it Andi Gentile? She had dark brown hair. Or maybe Jacqui Grant — the movie hopper — who has dark red hair. That was more likely. Jacqui always flirted with Robert. Still, it could be Andi. I recalled how Robert had smiled at her the other day.

Before I knew it, it was time to vote on whether we thought Abby could handle the role of interim president. Mary Anne handed out slips of paper and we all took pencils from a cup on Claudia's desk. I voted yes. Abby seemed perfectly capable, even if she was a little overeager. After all, it was just for a week.

We gave the folded slips to Mary Anne. She counted six yes votes and one no vote written in Kristy's distinctive, neat handwriting.

"Way to go!" Abby cheered. "Thanks guys. You won't be sorry. I've been thinking about coming up with some great new project to breathe some life into this club. I'm going to think about it tonight and come up with something truly great! I'll call you all tomorrow and let you know what it is."

As everyone left, they said good-bye to Kristy and wished her a great vacation. To her credit, Kristy shook Abby's hand and wrote down the name of the hotel where she'd be in Hawaii. "You can call me there if you need me," she said.

"Thanks, but I don't think I will," Abby replied.

When everyone left, I stayed behind. "What

are you going to do?" Claudia asked, her face concerned and sympathetic.

"Spy," I said decisively.

"What?" Claudia cried.

"I have to know what's really going on with Robert," I said as I got off the bed and started pacing the room.

"Ask him," Claudia suggested.

"What if he lies to me again?" I replied. "He already has once. I can't leave for New York without knowing. Want to do some spying with me?"

"Not particularly," Claudia replied.

"All right, then I'll do it myself."

"Okay, okay," Claudia relented. "I'll go with you. What good is a best friend if she won't spy with you?"

"Thanks." I didn't like the idea of spying on Robert, either. But I had no choice. If I didn't learn the truth about this, I was going to go crazy.

CHAPTER 5

Thursday

I can't beleeve I am riting in the notbook after Abby sade we didn't haf to, but I am. I haf to tell aboat wat happend the other day. We all no the Barrett and DeWitt kids can be wild. But I think they topped themselfs this time. Poor Abby! On her furst day as presitent, to!

Abby did come up with a fun idea for the club to get involved in. On Thursday morning, she called me and told me what it was. Her sister, Anna, is involved with an orphanage in Mexico. Anna's music class sends the children tapes of music they have performed. The kids from the orphanage write back. So, Abby's idea was for the BSC to put on a Mexican festival to raise money for the orphanage. She thought it would be something in which we could involve the kids we baby-sit for.

I said it sounded great to me but I wouldn't be in Stoneybrook on the day she wanted to hold the festival. Abby said she knew but she wondered if I wanted to get together that day to start working on it. "After all, I have to pull this off while I'm still president," she said with a laugh.

I said I really couldn't. Robert had called me that morning and wanted to go for a bike ride. I had told him I'd go, although I had no idea what it would be like now that I knew he had lied to me.

Abby then asked if she could spend money from the treasury for craft supplies. "I want to make *piñatas* for the festival," she told me.

I knew how much money was in there, so I told her she could take twenty dollars. "I think we should hang on to the rest of the money," I said, "especially since you won't be collecting dues while I'm away."

"Yes, but we won't be paying Charlie to drive," she reminded me. "So how about another ten? Thirty dollars would buy what we need."

"All right," I said. In her own way, Abby was as dynamic and persuasive as Kristy.

The bike outing with Robert that afternoon didn't go very well. I thought I was being myself, but Robert kept asking me what was wrong. Each time I said "Nothing." Somehow I just couldn't come out and confront him. I wanted to, but I was too chicken. What if he became insulted because I didn't trust him? What if he gave me an answer I didn't believe? I didn't want to go away for a week if things between us weren't right. So I left my questions unasked.

As soon as I came home, the phone rang. It was Claudia and she was dying to tell me what had happened during their first day of planning for the festival.

On short notice, Abby had managed to pull together a small crew of kids and BSC members to start preparations for the festival. They met at the old barn behind Mary Anne's house.

That worked out fine for Mary Anne and Claudia, since they were scheduled to baby-sit for Mrs. DeWitt. (There are seven kids in the DeWitt family, so Mary Anne and Claudia were sharing the job.) Mary Anne simply asked Mrs. DeWitt to drive the kids to her house instead of Mary Anne and Claudia going over there. "Glad to," Mrs. DeWitt told Mary Anne. "The kids are going bonkers with boredom. I can't wait until school starts. They'd love to get out of the house."

When Mrs. DeWitt remarried, she went from three kids to seven! They are: Buddy (eight), Suzi (five), and Marnie (two) (their last names are Barrett); Lindsey (eight), Taylor (six), Madeleine (four) and Ryan (two) (they're DeWitts). Can you imagine having two two-year-olds?

Anyway, Mrs. DeWitt drove the kids to the barn in her van. "Good luck!" she told Mary Anne and Claudia as the kids filed out of the van.

A few minutes later, Mallory arrived with her brothers and sisters. Then Jessi came with Becca. That day Abby was baby-sitting for Haley and Matt Braddock, who are nine and seven. She brought them along, and soon everyone was assembled in the barn, ready to create *piñatas*.

Abby laid out the materials she'd brought along: papier-mâché powder, strips of craft balsa wood, pipe cleaners, masking tape, glue, crepe paper, construction paper, paint, markers, and fabric paint. She even had a bag of plastic swirly eyeballs. "You bought all that for thirty dollars?" Claudia said.

"Fifty. I threw in twenty of my own," Abby said as she pulled a thick book titled *Party Crafts* from the bag. "It says right here how to do everything."

Mary Anne found some rubber tubs in the barn and dragged in the garden hose. Abby ripped open the bag of papier-mâché with such zeal that everyone around her was lightly powdered with the stuff. Naturally Claudia, with her artistic flair, threw herself into the project. "You pour the powder while I pour the water," she instructed Abby. "The thickness has to be just right or it doesn't work."

While they poured and mixed, Mary Anne went into her house and found a stack of newspapers in the family's recycling bin. "This is an unusual form of recycling," she said as she returned to the barn and set the stack down. "But it *is* recycling."

"Sure it is, and for a good cause," Abby replied, stirring the grayish-white papier-mâché glop.

Abby, Claudia, Mary Anne, Mallory, and Jessi helped the kids create the frameworks for their *piñatas* using balsa wood, pipe cleaners, masking tape, and some glue. Becca, Haley, and Vanessa got together to work on a unicorn. Matt joined Nicky and the triplets to work on a *piñata* jet plane. Margo and Claire decided to make a teddy bear. And the Barrett and DeWitt kids teamed up to make a big dragon.

Claudia smiled as she watched the Barretts and DeWitts work, with Buddy and Lindsey directing things. Those two families of kids hadn't blended so well at first. But now they seemed to be getting along great.

"This was a good idea," Claudia told Abby. "It's working out really well."

Abby grinned. "Piece of cake. See? You don't have to be a tyrant to make things work. Kristy turns everything into a major scene, like it has to be planned down to the last tiny detail."

"Well, things don't always run as smoothly as this," Claudia said. "Sometimes we're really glad she keeps things under control."

Abby spread her arms, gesturing toward the group. "Everything's under control, isn't it? No problemo."

As their older siblings worked on the dragon, Marnie and Ryan discovered the joy of squishing their fingers in the gloppy papier-mâché. They were having such a ball that Claudia let them do it for a few minutes. But then they started smearing it in their hair and on their clothing. "That's enough," Claudia said, steering them away from the tubs. "Go help work on the dragon."

"No, they'll wreck everything," Suzi complained as the sticky toddlers headed toward the dragon.

Claudia gave Marnie and Ryan a quick course in being gentle to the dragon, taking their hands and softly patting it. "See?" she said. "Nice dragon. Gentle!"

"Roarrrr!" Marnie shouted, sending Ryan off in a gale of laughter.

Within half an hour, the forms were done and the kids started to wet their newspaper strips and lay them across the forms they'd created. This was when things began to get just the teeniest bit out of control.

The paper strips stuck to their hands and sleeves. Unknown to him, Nicky was now dragging around a long sticky tail, which Byron had stuck to the back of his pants. A paper strip wrapped itself around Margo's shoe. She struggled with it as if it were some kind of snake wrapping itself around her foot. At one point Claudia wouldn't have been surprised if the kids wound up looking like living mummies.

But, as time went on, the *piñatas* began taking shape, and they were coming out very well. (Most of them, anyway. Margo and

Claire's bear was extremely lopsided.)

"Our dragon rules," Taylor boasted as he worked on bringing its long tail to a point. "It's the best one."

"Is not," cried Vanessa. "Dragons drool and unicorns rule!"

"No way!" Buddy protested. "That unicorn looks like a donkey."

"Does not!" Becca shouted back.

"They're all terrific." Abby stepped in to defuse the argument. "You're all doing a great job."

"Dragons rule, dragons rule," Taylor mumbled stubbornly.

"I'd better get more newspaper," Mary Anne said, heading for the door. "Want me to open this door, anyone? It's warm in here."

"Yeah, open it," Mallory said. "The smell of that papier-mâché is getting to me."

Mary Anne pushed the door open, letting in a flood of afternoon sunshine and a gentle breeze.

"That breeze will help dry the paper," said Claudia, who was now working on the teddy bear with Margo and Claire.

"Marnie! Stop!" Madeleine complained. Marnie was pulling off the triangular scales Madeleine was trying to glue to the dragon's back. "Someone make her stop!"

"Go away, Marnie," said Buddy as he

worked on the dragon's face. "You're making a mess."

"Marnie, stop!" said Jessi, Mallory, Abby, and Claudia, all at once. Wide-eyed at being the center of so much attention, Marnie put her hands to her face and smeared it with papier-mâché.

"Eeewww! Gross!" shouted Madeleine.

Claudia laughed and swept Marnie up in her arms, wiping her face. At the same time Ryan yanked at the hem of her shirt. "Up! Up!" he cried, holding his arms up. Claudia set Marnie down and picked up Ryan.

Just then, Margo and Claire let out a horrified yowl. "Teddy!" Claire shrieked as their papier-mâché *piñata* toppled to the right, caving in.

"It's ruined!" Margo wailed.

"We can fix it," Claudia assured her as she set Ryan down. Ryan toddled off and Claudia righted the fallen teddy. She set to work reuniting his broken balsa wood frame with pieces of masking tape. Then she overlaid the repaired frame with strips of papier-mâché. When she was done, Teddy looked better than he had before his fall.

"Thank you so, so, so much," Claire said, hugging Claudia.

"You're welcome." Claudia stood and blew a strand of hair from her face and wiped her gloppy hands on her denim shorts. With her artist's eye, she surveyed the scene around her. Everyone was working diligently on the *piñatas*, quiet and absorbed in the project, at least for the moment. Colorful scraps of paper dotted the earth colors of the barn. A shaft of bright sunlight streamed through the open door. Claudia wished she'd brought her pastels and a pad so she could sketch the scene in color.

But, as she planned her sketch, she became aware that something was making her uneasy. What was it? Scanning the area, she tried to imagine what it could be. Then she realized. "Where's Marnie?" she asked, her eyes darting to every corner of the barn. "Has anyone seen Marnie?"

Jessi looked up from the newspaper she was tearing into strips. "She was standing next to Buddy a minute ago."

"Buddy?" Claudia cried, fighting her panic.

Buddy shrugged. "I haven't seen her."

"Me neither," said Lindsey.

Claudia looked at the open door. Could Marnie have run out while no one was watching? She dashed into the yard. "Marnie! Marnie!"

"Not here?" asked Abby, coming out of the barn behind her. Claudia shook her head. Abby bounded past her to Burnt Hill Road and looked in both directions. "Ma-a-a-a-rniiieee!"

As Claudia wondered what to do next, Mary Anne returned carrying another stack of newspapers. "What's wrong?"

"We can't find — " Claudia began, but Abby cut her off, grabbing Mary Anne's arm.

"Come back to the house with me, come on!" she said frantically. "We have to call nine-one-one. Marnie is missing."

Mary Anne paled. "Marnie is — " Abby didn't let her finish. She tugged at Mary Anne's arm, causing her to drop the pile of papers at Claudia's feet.

Claudia watched them run toward the house. Her heart banged like a jackhammer. What had happened? Had Marnie been kidnapped? The thought made her dizzy with fright.

"Any luck?" Jessi called from the barn doorway.

Just as Claudia turned toward her, the sound of terrible screaming came from the barn. Claudia ran back inside.

"It's alive!" Claire shrieked, pointing at the dragon. "It moved. I saw it!"

Then Margo screamed and grabbed her sister in a tight, frightened hug.

"It did move!" Becca shouted, pointing. "I saw it, too!"

With that, Lindsey, Buddy, Taylor, and Suzi

exploded into peals of hysterical laughter. "You fell for it!" Buddy howled.

Lindsey held her side as she laughed. "I don't believe you! How dumb can you be?"

Taylor and Suzi were laughing so hard they had to hold each other up.

The dragon moved again and a noise came from inside. On a hunch, Claudia gingerly lifted the dragon. Marnie was beneath it.

She pouted and looked close to tears. "Poor Marnie," said Claudia, picking her up. She was upset with Buddy and Lindsey. They should have known better. But she could also understand how a kid might think this was funny.

Suddenly, Claudia gasped. Abby was calling 911.

Claudia handed Marnie to Jessi. "I'll be right back," she called, running for the door. She darted across the yard to Mary Anne's kitchen door.

"I'm not sure what she was wearing," Abby was saying into the phone. "Yes, she's two."

"We found her!" Claudia said, panting.

Abby took the phone away from her ear. "You what?"

"She's all right." Claudia gasped, falling into a chair.

"Oh, thank goodness," Mary Anne said.

Abby turned back to the phone. "We found

her. I'm very sorry. She's all right. . . . No, really. We don't need assistance. . . . I'm sure. . . . Okay. Thanks."

Claudia told them what had happened. Abby leaned heavily against the kitchen counter. "Oh, man. That was close. Really close."

"Maybe we were trying to do too much," Mary Anne suggested. "You know, it's a big project to do with so many kids, especially little kids."

Claudia told me she agreed with Mary Anne. Kristy probably would have insisted that they have more sitters for that many kids. Or that each sitter had to stay with a particular group, or something else which would have kept them from getting disorganized and losing sight of a kid.

"Boy, was that scary," Abby said.

"I told you things don't always run that smoothly," Claudia reminded her.

"This was just one of those things," Abby objected. "It could have happened to anyone."

But Claudia wondered about that. Somehow, she couldn't picture it happening to Kristy.

CHAPTER 6

On Friday, my opportunity to spy on Robert came. I called his house in the morning and his mother told me he'd gone to the movies at Washington Mall.

All kinds of suspicion bells started ringing for me. The day before on our bike ride he hadn't mentioned it. Normally he would have said something like, "I'll be going to the movies with some guys tomorrow. See you in the afternoon." But he hadn't. He'd just kissed me lightly and said, "See you later."

Immediately, I called Claudia. "Operation Robert is on," I announced.

"Stacey, this is so dumb," she complained. "Do we really have to?"

"You promised," I reminded her.

"Oh, all right."

We took the half-hour bus ride to the mall and entered the main lobby. "Will you take off those sunglasses, please," Claudia said to me as the lobby fountain sprayed pink water into the air behind us. "Do you really think you're going to fool Robert? He's seen you in sunglasses before. It's not as if he wouldn't recognize you."

I took off the glasses. "All right. But if we're going to spy on Robert, we have to do it right." I pulled a list from the pocket of my flowered sundress. "Here's where we should look for him. I say we start at Critters. Robert likes the iguanas. He thinks they're cool but his mother won't let him have one."

Claudia read the list over my shoulder. "I think we should check out Cinema World first," she said. "That way we can see if any movie Robert would like is playing, check out the time, and then make sure we're there when people are going in."

"Brilliant!" I said, heading toward the escalator. We took it to the fourth floor and then went to Cinema World. Two movies Robert had mentioned wanting to see were listed on the marquee outside the theater. "I don't know which one he'd choose," I admitted, peering up at the signs.

"We'll come back for the first one, and if he's not there, we'll come back fifteen minutes later for the next one," said Claudia sensibly.

We checked BookCenter and Critters and then came back for the twelve-thirty showing of *Hang Tough*, a movie in which a lot of things blow up. Robert loves movies like that, but we never see them together because they're not my kind of movie. We lingered outside the theater, watching people buy tickets. Suddenly, I spotted Robert walking toward the theater with a Power Records bag in his hand. I grabbed Claudia and ducked into the store next to the theater.

Robert stood in front of the theater, looking around as if he were waiting for someone to arrive. I nearly held my breath as I craned my neck out of the doorway, waiting to see who would show up. If it was a girl, what would I do? I had no idea.

Claudia was at my shoulder, also trying to see without being seen. She let out a low laugh.

"What?" I whispered, turning to her.

"Look who's coming to meet Robert," she said, smiling.

"Pete," I said, feeling everything inside me relax. It was Pete Black. He goes to SMS with us. I sort of dated him for awhile, but now we're just friends.

"He looks good with his hair long," Claudia observed. Over the summer Pete had grown his brown hair. It was now down over the collar of his denim shirt.

I leaned in the doorway and smiled. "Of

course," I said. "I never want to see shoot 'em up, blow 'em up kinds of movies with him, so he's going with a guy friend. That makes sense."

"But does Robert usually hang out with Pete?" Claudia asked.

"They know each other pretty well," I said. "He doesn't hang out with Marty Bukowski, either, but supposedly he played basketball with him the other day. That's what he says, anyway. Maybe his story is partly true. Maybe he played basketball with Marty and went to the mall? Maybe Robert is trying to expand his horizons by hanging out with Marty or something." As soon as I used the term *expand his horizons* I started worrying all over again. What if he wanted to expand his girlfriend horizons, too?

I peeked at the front of the theater again, but Robert and Pete had already gone inside. The two people I saw standing there instead made me clutch Claudia's arm. Two beautiful-looking girls of about fifteen or sixteen stood in front as if they were waiting for someone.

"What's the matter now?" Claudia asked.

"Those girls," I said. "What if Robert and Pete are double-dating them?"

"They're in high school," Claudia said doubtfully.

"So? Older women sometimes date younger men!"

"Stacey! Get a grip!"

The girls turned toward the box office window and bought tickets to *Hang Tough*. "That proves it!" I exclaimed, stepping out of the doorway. "Two girls would never go see *that* movie unless they were meeting guys. I bet anything they're meeting Pete and Robert."

"They might go see it on their own," Claudia disagreed. "I don't know, Stacey."

"Come on," I said, already charging toward the movie theater. "I have to know." I reached the window before Claudia and bought us two tickets to *Hang Tough*. Claudia and I arrived at the entrance to the movie in time to see the backs of the girls as they went in. I waited just a moment, then entered the dark theater, pulling Claudia in with me.

"Look, Claud," I whispered, peering down the center aisle.

Halfway down the aisle, I could see the silhouettes of the girls. Each girl had met up with a boy. My worst suspicion was true.

All I could see was the backs of their heads, but I was positive the boys were Pete and Robert. Claudia and I found two seats about ten rows back from where they sat with their dates.

We sat through the entire movie — every last bomb blast of it. Through the thundering explosions I kept my eye on the couples. Luckily, there was no kissing or anything like that going on. (I might have lost it altogether if there had been.) But just as the hero, Brad Wallace, was saving everyone, Claudia turned to me and said, "I just noticed something. That's not Pete's new hair."

"What?" I asked.

"Pete's hair is long now. Those two guys up there have short hair."

I jumped up to get a better look. She was right! "Sit down," hissed the woman behind me.

"Sorry," I apologized as I stepped into the aisle. Without thinking, I walked right down to where the couples were sitting. The girls were not with Robert and Pete after all! I walked up and down the aisle, checking everyone. The boys weren't even in this theater. "Let's go," I whispered, leaning in to Claudia.

"I want to see the end," she protested. "We sat through it this far."

"Everything blows up but nobody dies," I said. "They all end the same. Now, come on." With a reluctant groan, Claudia stood up and followed me out of the theater. I looked at all the other movies playing. Where could Pete and Robert be?

From behind me, a door opened. "Stacey!"

I whirled around. "Robert!"

"Hi, Pete," Claudia said, sounding sheepish and looking very guilty.

"Hi, guys," Pete replied.

Glancing at the doorway, I saw that Robert and Pete had been watching a romantic Julie Talbert movie that I had really wanted to see. "I thought we were going to see that together," I said.

"You're going away next week, and by the time you come back it won't be playing any longer," he said. "What did you see?"

"That," Claudia said, pointing to the *Hang Tough* sign.

Robert looked at me as if I'd gone nuts. "Since when do you want to see a movie like *Hang Tough*?"

"Uh . . . Claudia wanted to see it," I lied.

"Yes. I love movies like that." Claudia backed me up with a nervous giggle. "The more bombs the better."

Pete and Robert exchanged puzzled glances. They knew something wasn't right, but they weren't sure what. "Well, we're all here now," Robert said, shrugging off his confusion. "Want to grab some lunch?"

"Sure," I replied. We decided to eat at Friendly's. Lunch was fun. Pete and Robert clowned around. Everyone was in a good mood. I was certainly relieved that Robert hadn't been on a double date with a high school girl.

As we left Friendly's, Pete and Robert said they were going to go play video games. Claudia and I wanted to go to Zingy's, a store where they sell cool clothes. We agreed to go our separate ways. "Want to play tennis this evening?" I asked Robert just before Claudia and I went into Zingy's.

A cornered look came into Robert's eyes. "Uh . . . Pete and I were going to . . . to . . . play baseball with some guys."

"We can come watch," I suggested.

"No . . . it's Pete's cousins. They live over in Lawrenceville," Robert said.

"I don't think there's any more room in the van," Pete added.

I nodded. "Okay. But I'm leaving tomorrow. I guess I won't see you then until I get back," I said, feeling hurt.

"I'll come by in the morning," said Robert. "We can go to the train station together."

That made me feel a little better. "Okay. Give me a call tonight."

"Okay. So long."

Claudia and I stood in front of Zingy's and watched them walk away. "See?" Claudia said. "Everything turned out okay."

"I'm not sure," I said thoughtfully. "Did you believe that baseball story?"

"Yeah, why not?"

"I don't know. Robert seemed nervous. And how come he's suddenly spending so much time with Pete Black?"

"They're becoming better friends?" Claudia suggested.

"Maybe," I agreed. "Or maybe he's not really going to be with Pete tonight. What if he's just using Pete as a cover?"

"No," Claudia said. Then she frowned. "Do you think?"

"I don't know," I replied, sighing. "But something isn't right. I can feel it." I didn't like the feeling, either. Not one bit.

CHAPTER 7

By eleven o'clock Saturday morning, I still hadn't heard from Robert. "Stacey, we've got to get going," Mom said. "Otherwise you'll miss the eleven-forty-five train."

"Just one minute, okay?" I pleaded. I went to the kitchen phone and called Robert. His mother answered.

"Sorry, Stacey, he left about an hour ago and I'm not sure where he went," she told me.

"All right. Thanks." I hung up with a lump in my throat. Had he forgotten I was leaving this morning?

Mom came into the kitchen. "Your father will be waiting for you at Grand Central Station and he's expecting you on the — " She stopped when she saw my expression. "What's the matter, Stacey?"

"I was expecting Robert to come by before I left but he must have forgotten."

"I'm sorry, honey."

"It's okay," I said, sniffing back the urge to cry. "Let's go." I'd left my suitcase in the living room. It weighed a ton since Mom and I had gone all out during our back-to-school shop-athon at Bellair's. With a grunt, I lifted the suitcase and opened the front door.

And there was Robert, one hand poised to ring the bell, the other holding the biggest bouquet of flowers — white daisies, yellow sunflowers, and orange daylilies — I'd ever seen.

"Robert!" I cried, putting down my suitcase.

"These are for you," he said, handing me the flowers.

"They're beautiful!" I cried. "Thank you so much. You are so sweet!"

"Take them with you to the city," Mom suggested, smiling as she came up behind me in the doorway. "Just put them in water when you arrive at your father's."

"Okay," I agreed. I would have hated to have left them behind. "Come on, Robert. Take a ride with us to the station."

Robert agreed. He carried my suitcase to the car and put it in the trunk. "I thought you'd forgotten I was leaving," I said as we climbed into the backseat.

"No way. Sorry I'm late, though. The flower

stand was mobbed. Everybody in the world was buying flowers today," he explained.

"That's all right. You made it in time," I said as Mom started the engine. I was just so happy he was there. I couldn't have stood going away with things uneasy between us. "How was the baseball game last night?"

"Oh, great," he said. I waited for more details, but he just smiled at me.

"You're sure getting to be friendly with Pete," I commented.

"Yeah," he agreed. "Pete's a good guy."

Something about these vague answers made me uncomfortable. But I didn't want anything to spoil our last moments together. When we arrived at the station I bought my ticket. "You and Robert wait out on the platform," Mom suggested, taking her cellular phone from her purse. "I want to call work and check on something."

"Okay," I agreed, kissing Mom's cheek. I knew she was just giving Robert and me time alone. Mom can be very cool that way. "I'll see you in a week."

Robert and I walked out onto the long platform. Only a few other people were there. He put down my suitcase and I rested the flowers on it. "Have a good time," he said, taking my hands in his.

In the distance, a whistle blew. We turned and looked at the approaching train. "I'll miss you," I said.

"Me, too," Robert replied, nodding.

I felt so close to him. I wanted to ask him — straight out — who he'd had lunch with at Casa Grande the other day. But this moment was perfect. I couldn't stand to spoil it.

The train pulled into the station and we hugged. It was a long, emotional hug.

"All aboard," the conductor shouted. "Express train to Grand Central Station. All aboard!"

"I'd better go," I said. Robert picked up my suitcase and got on the train long enough to throw it into an overhead rack for me. With a quick kiss on the lips, he hurried off the train just as the doors slid shut behind him.

Taking a window seat, I looked out and waved to Robert. He saw me and waved back. The train started moving. I kept waving until Robert was very small. He kept waving, too.

I felt sad, though I didn't know why. I would be gone for just one week. What was the big deal? Robert and I were probably being overdramatic.

Sitting back in my seat, I shut my eyes. What was I sad about? Was it that I'd miss Robert? Or was it that I was afraid I was losing him? It was so confusing. Something was up with him. Yet he'd come to see me off with flowers, hadn't he? And he'd looked upset, too.

I wondered again who he'd been with at Casa Grande. Could Emily have gotten it wrong? Or what if it was the back of Pete Black, with his new long hair, that she'd seen? But, if so, why would he lie about it? Why had he said he was playing basketball with Marty Bukowski?

I wondered and worried about these things almost all the way to the city. I'd brought a magazine to read, but I was too distracted by my own concerns to focus on it.

Yet, when the train entered a tunnel and everything outside went black, something inside me changed — just as it always does when I enter that tunnel. To me, the tunnel is a signal that the train will be pulling into the station very soon.

My city self takes over in that tunnel. I feel faster. More sophisticated. In some ways, I even feel smarter. It's hard to describe, but there's a change.

By the time the train pulled into one of the many bulb-lit underground platforms in Grand Central Station I wasn't feeling sad about Robert anymore. I was thinking about the city and how much fun this week would be.

"All out for Grand Central," the conductor's

voice came over the P.A. system. "Last stop. Remember to take your valuables. Last stop."

I reached up and struggled to get my suitcase off the rack. "Want help?" asked a man with a beard. Before I could answer, he lifted the suitcase down and handed it to me. City people have a reputation for being cold and unfriendly. But I don't think that's so at all. I've never found them to be that way.

With my huge bouquet of flowers stuck under one arm, I dragged my suitcase down the aisle and out the door. In the waiting area, I looked around at the sea of people. In minutes, I spotted my father. "Dad!" I called, waving.

He saw me right away and hurried through the crowd. "How's my girl?" he asked, wrapping me in a hug.

"Great," I replied. Despite my worries over Robert, I did feel great. I was so glad to be in the city with my father.

"Who gave you flowers?" he asked.

"Robert."

"Hey, you're blushing!" he teased.

"I am not!" I insisted, though I probably was.

"Are you hungry?"

"Sort of."

"Good. I thought we'd eat at the Oyster Bar."

"All right!" I cheered. The Oyster Bar is a restaurant right in Grand Central on the lower level. They serve mostly fish and shellfish. Not only do I like the food, but, to me, the Oyster Bar is *very* New York.

"We'll do lots of fun things this week," Dad said.

"I can't wait," I told him. It was great to be back in New York.

CHAPTER 8

Saturday

Sorry if it uses up a lot of paper, but I like writing in the club notebook. Considering the amount of money we out and out wasted making signs for our festival, I don't see why it should matter. What's the cost of a few notebooks when we practically threw thirty dollars worth of art supplies in the trash ?!

Mallory phoned me at Dad's apartment that night. "Help!" she said. "Abby is a lunatic! She's ruining the club!"

"Calm down," I told her. "What happened?"

Apparently, Abby had called another special meeting in order to make signs advertising the Mexican festival. Once again, the kids met at Dawn's and Mary Anne's barn.

This time, Mary Anne was baby-sitting for Sara and Norman Hill, who are nine and seven. Sara, who loves art, was very excited about working on the project. Claudia arrived with Charlotte Johanssen (eight), and Jessi came with Becca again. Charlotte and Becca are best friends, so they were thrilled to see each other. This time Mallory showed up with only Vanessa, Margo, and Claire, since the boys were playing baseball somewhere.

Abby came last with the Rodowsky kids whom she was sitting for: Shea (nine), Jackie (seven), and Archie (four). "Everyone owes me six dollars," she announced as she set a paper bag on the ground in the barn.

"What for?" Mallory asked.

"I spent thirty-six bucks on these supplies. Six times six is thirty-six, so you each owe me six."

"Since we're all paying for the supplies,

shouldn't we have talked about it first?" Mallory protested, trying to be diplomatic.

"I'm president, aren't I?" Abby replied. "*And* treasurer. I make those decisions."

Mallory didn't know how to argue this point, but it didn't seem right to her.

"The treasurer and president make decisions about money that we've already contributed in dues," Claudia said. "You can't just charge us for stuff you decide to buy."

Abby faced Claudia, hands on hips. Her expression was annoyed. The fact that all the kids were staring at Abby, Claudia, and Mallory made it even more tense. "Forget it," Abby said with a smile and a shrug. "I'll eat the other thirty myself. It's no big deal."

"You shouldn't have to do that," Mary Anne said quickly. "That wouldn't be fair to you." She took a five-dollar bill from the back pocket of her jeans, added a single to it, and handed it to Abby.

"Thanks," Abby said.

Mallory still didn't think it was fair to have to pay for something she hadn't agreed to buy, but she felt she ought to offer the money since Mary Anne had. She fished six singles from her pocket, as did Jessi and Claudia. "Next time ask me before you buy art supplies. I have a ton of stuff I could have brought over," Claudia grumbled.

"Sure. Okay," Abby agreed. "I'll try to remember I'm a president and not a dictator."

Claudia laughed. "Good idea."

With that done, Abby set to work laying out sheets of posterboard, markers, glitter pens, crayons, and paint. "Okay, guys," she said to the group. "The festival is next Saturday. We'll start at noon. There will be games, food, and fun. We'll hold it at . . ." She looked around. "Where?"

"You mean you don't know?" Mallory asked.

"I figured I'd come up with someplace," Abby answered.

"I thought it was going to be at your house," Jessi said.

"We could have it there. But it's sort of out of the way. How about the schoolyard?"

"I could call the school board president and ask for permission," Mary Anne offered. "It's short notice, though. And what would we write on the posters?"

"I know," Abby said. "You go inside and try to call the school board president and we'll leave that part blank until we hear from you."

"Okay," Mary Anne agreed. "I think Sharon has the president's number somewhere."

(Sharon is Dawn's mother, Mary Anne's step-mother.)

Mary Anne left and the kids spread out, each with a piece of posterboard. "Make sure you say that this is a BSC festival," Abby told the kids. "That way people know it's going to be good."

"How do you spell it?" asked Archie.

"Spell what?" Claudia asked him.

"I don't know," Archie answered with a shrug. "I can't spell anything."

"Spell Mexican," Margo requested.

Claudia sighed and frowned, thinking hard. "I'd better do that," Mallory jumped in. She could just imagine the creative spelling Claudia would come up with.

For the next hour, the kids worked on their posters. Norman, who is overweight (though he's dieting), filled the board with pictures of tacos, chili, burritos, and tortillas. "That's nice artwork, Norman, but there's no room left for writing," Jessi pointed out gently.

"Oops," said Norman, absently brushing blue paint through his wispy blond hair. "Could I have another board?" There was one extra board, so Jessi gave it to him.

His sister, Sara, drew a great burro with a colorful Mexican *serape* on its back. She wrote BSC Mexican Fe — in huge letters, and then decided she had run out of room. Claudia helped her fit the rest in. When they were done it said:

BSC Mexican Festuval.
Gaems, Foode, and Fun.
Nexd Sadurday
at no one.

"Nice spelling," Mallory said, looking down at Claudia and Sara as they worked.

Claudia looked up and chewed on her lip anxiously. "Not even close?"

"Close but . . ." Mallory got on her knees and tried to fix the spelling mistakes with a marker as neatly as she could.

"Hey, cut it out!" Becca shouted at Jackie, who was shooting globs of glitter onto her arm from a glitter pen.

Abby took the pen from him. "Try not to waste the glitter," she told him. "We don't have a lot of it."

"Yuck! It's all over me!" Becca complained, wiping a smear of gold glitter down her arm.

"Smear it on your poster," Abby suggested.

In fifteen minutes, Mary Anne returned to the barn. "No luck," she reported. "The school can't let us use the schoolyard because of insurance. I asked Sharon, though, and she said we could have it here."

"Cool!" Abby exclaimed. "Everybody write that the festival will be here."

"Where is here?" Charlotte asked.

"One seventy-seven Burnt Hill Road," Mary Anne told her.

Mallory checked her watch and saw that they'd already been there about an hour. "We have to be home in an hour to go visit my uncle," she said.

"I'm supposed to get these guys back by then, too," Abby said, frowning as she looked at the posters. "Okay, everybody. We have to pick up speed here. The first person done gets to keep the markers and the crayons. Ready, set, go!"

The kids started writing and drawing furiously. Crayons actually flew into the air as they were finished with them. "You can slow down a little," Mallory advised, nervous about what this frenzy of activity might produce.

"Done!" Shea Rodowski announced in about ten minutes.

"Let's see," Claudia said skeptically. Shea held up a swirl of scribble-scrabble with letters mixed up in it. "I can't read it," she said.

One by one Shea picked out all the letters to the words. They were all there, only impossible for anyone else to understand. "I win," he announced.

"No fair," Vanessa protested. "His is a mess!"

"Oh, yeah? Let's see yours," Shea challenged her.

Vanessa's was also hastily thrown together. In the center of a colorful blur of glitter, a poem was written in tiny script. "I'll read it," she declared. "Come to the Mexican fest. The food will be the best. Games galore and much, much more. So put it to the test."

"Nice," said Abby, "but you don't say where or when."

"Oh, they'll figure that out," Vanessa insisted.

"How?" Mallory asked, rolling her eyes.

"People talk," Vanessa said. "Or they can go look at another sign."

"I finished first, so I win," Shea said, collecting the pens and crayons.

Sara gathered her markers and crayons defensively. "You can't have them yet! I'm not done making a border."

"Wait until everyone's finished," Abby told Shea. "You all have ten more minutes, then we have to go and hang them up."

When the ten minutes were up, Mallory couldn't believe how messy the signs were. The writing was either sloppy, nearly illegible, or too small to read. The words were full of misspellings. Some of the artwork was cute, but a lot of it had been done too quickly, dashed off in order to win the crayons and markers.

Abby gathered up the signs. Mallory wanted to say that they were too awful to put up, but she didn't want to offend the kids. Jessi, Claudia, and Mary Anne also looked concerned; they probably felt the same as Mallory.

Mal thought about Kristy and could easily imagine *her* speaking up. "No way," she would say. "It would be totally embarrassing to put those up!" She might say it in private when the kids wouldn't hear, but she'd certainly say it.

Mallory felt that in Kristy's absence someone should say something. She couldn't get up the nerve to do it, though. Perhaps she was being too critical. The posters might not really be as bad as she thought.

The group split up, with each baby-sitter taking a bunch of kids around to put up signs. They hung them on trees and electric poles. At the end of the hour, they returned to the barn. "Well, that's done," Abby said, brushing her hands together.

Just then Mr. and Mrs. Pike pulled up in the family's minivan to pick up the girls. Mallory didn't think about the signs again until after supper when Abby called. "We have to collect all the signs," she said. "Anna and my mother think they look terrible."

"No kidding," Mallory said wryly.

"What? You thought so, too? Why didn't you say something?"

"You're the president!" Mal exploded.

"Yeah, well . . . I was just anxious to get them up, but I took down all the ones I could find. If you see any more, just yank them off."

"What will we do for signs?" Mallory asked.

"I'll make them," Abby volunteered.

"Are we going to have to pay for more supplies?" Mallory asked.

"No. I'll borrow them from Claudia, I guess."

"Okay. 'Bye." Mallory hung up and then called me in the city. She couldn't believe they'd wasted the day and the money for the supplies. "Besides, anyone who already saw the signs probably thinks we're crazy. Abby is fun and I like her a lot, but we need Kristy back," she said to me. "And we need her BAAAD!"

CHAPTER 9

On Sunday, Dad and I took a cab from his apartment on East 65th Street to the Metropolitan Museum of Art on the east side of Central Park. I just love the Met. There is always so much to see.

Dad was interested in a special exhibit of medieval armor which I can't say thrilled me. "So," he asked as we wandered through the cases of gleaming breastplates, helmets, and swords, "how's everything with you?"

"Good," I said. "I guess."

"You guess?" Dad leaned toward a case for a closer look at a metal boot.

I studied my reflection in the glass. In a strange way, I didn't recognize the person staring back at me. The person in the glass looked older than I remembered. Maybe it was just a trick of the light, or the sophisticated museum setting in the background.

"You don't sound certain," Dad said, studying me.

"Um . . . no, I'm sure. It's just that Robert has been acting weird lately."

Dad frowned. "Weird? In what way?"

"I don't know. . . . I feel like there's something he's not telling me."

"Like what?"

"If I knew I wouldn't be worried about it," I replied.

Dad nodded and we walked on to the next case. We continued looking at the armor without talking until we got to the end of the exhibit. "Now where to?" he asked.

"The Egyptians?" I suggested. I visit the Egyptian section every time I come to the museum. I love the jewelry they wore, and those great headdresses.

"Okay," Dad agreed. We headed across the main lobby and over to the exhibit. The way you enter the exhibit is so cool. You walk through a small passage that resembles a pyramid doorway. Every time I go through it I imagine myself as an archaeologist discovering all that great stuff for the first time.

After passing by the same displays I'd seen a million times, I stopped at a small mummy lying in a stone sarcophagus. I hadn't remembered ever seeing it before. I bent down to read the card on the corner of the glass case surrounding the chipped, square, stone tomb. "Wow," I said to Dad who was by my side. "He was a pharaoh at only fourteen."

Dad nodded absently as if his mind was on something else. "You know, Stacey," he began. "About you and Robert . . . do you think you might be a little too young to be dating steadily?"

"No," I answered bluntly.

"I think maybe you are," he said thoughtfully. "You're only thirteen. That's awfully young."

I pointed at the mummy. "This guy here was only fourteen. And he was the pharaoh of all Egypt!" I said. I didn't like the direction this conversation was taking. Why was Dad saying this now? He'd known about Robert for a long time.

"This guy here was also dead at fourteen," Dad pointed out. "Most of the ancient Egyptians didn't live past forty. But you're going to live a lot longer than that. You'll meet a lot of people in your lifetime. You'll go to college and meet young men. You'll work, travel, and do all sorts of things. You'll meet a lot of people before you're even out of your twenties. Are you sure you want to limit yourself to only one boy when you're still so young?"

I regretted having said anything about Robert. Dad was probably saying all this because he thought Robert had upset me. He's very protective that way.

"Robert's a great guy," I said to set his mind at ease.

"I'm not saying he's not," Dad replied, as we walked down the hallway past the golden dog god statues, marble plaques covered with hieroglyphics, and the mummy cases. "Even if he were the greatest guy on Earth, I think you should meet others so you can compare."

"I don't want to compare," I grumbled.

"Why not?"

"Because Robert and I are perfect together."

"Are you sure?" Dad asked.

"Yes." We had come to the huge room where the temple of Dendur sits across a large pool. I took the opportunity to escape from Dad and his lecture. Acting as though I were wildly eager to get to the temple, I hurried toward it, leaving him standing in the entranceway.

As I climbed the wide stone steps to the temple, I realized how annoyed I was with him. What was he trying to do? Break up Robert and me? Just because his marriage hadn't worked out didn't mean he had the right to get between two people who were perfectly happy.

Me and my big mouth. Why did I have to

tell him about my worries anyway? He was probably saying all this now because I'd given him an opening. He figured I was concerned about things with Robert so he'd take the opportunity to make things worse. He wanted us to break up. He was saying we were too young because he thought I was still a little girl.

Dad caught up to me near one of the temple walls. "You're mad at me, aren't you?" he said.

I was startled. I thought I'd given him the slip in a subtle way. I looked around the small stone room and saw we were alone. "How could you tell?" I asked.

"Because you stomped away from me just now."

"I didn't stomp."

Dad laughed lightly. "I'd simply like you to consider what I've said. From what you told me earlier, it doesn't sound as if everything is so perfect between Robert and you. Things might go more smoothly with someone else."

"Things are fine the way they are," I told him firmly. "I'm just worried over nothing. Forget I said anything about it."

"You were the one who said he was lying to you."

"I said he was keeping something from me.

I did *not* say he was lying. You saw the flowers I brought with me to the city," I replied. "Those were from Robert. Remember? Would he have given me an expensive, humongous bouquet if there was a problem?"

I noticed that my voice was amplified and ringing in that small stone space. It made me realize how upset I sounded.

Dad looked at me for a moment. "I don't know," he said quietly. "We can forget about it for now. Okay?"

"Okay," I agreed, folding my arms. "Good."

We continued through the rest of the exhibit without much conversation. I suppose I was still mad, although I didn't want to be. But I couldn't help it. Dad wasn't supposed to say, "I don't know." He was supposed to say, "You're right, Stacey. The flowers mean everything is fine. I was wrong."

He made me feel as if I had to defend my relationship with Robert, as if something was wrong with it.

An hour later, we left the museum, still not talking naturally to each other. Dad tried a few times, but I just answered him stiffly. I wasn't ready to forget our argument.

Robert and I were right for each other, and nothing was going to change that — no matter what Dad thought.

CHAPTER 10

On Monday I woke up early, eager to see the Walkers. I heard the water running in the bathroom and knew Dad was getting ready for work. It's unusual for me to be with him on a weekday.

Things between Dad and me had smoothed out during the evening. We were friends again, although neither of us had mentioned Robert since our talk in the museum. We just sort of let the topic go away. Mom says Dad and I are both "nonconfrontational." That means we'd rather sidestep an issue than fight about it. She's right about that.

I looked through the new clothes Mom and I had bought. It was still awfully warm out. None of them were really right. I narrowed my choices down to a sundress I have with flowers all over it and a straight, black sleeveless dress. I decided the black one looked too dressy, so I went with the sundress.

As I walked out of my bedroom, Dad came out of the bathroom bundled in a white terrycloth robe. "I'm taking a cab to work. Want a lift to the Walkers'?"

"Sure," I replied.

"We'll pick up a bagel or something at the corner deli," he said.

"Great." Now that Dad's single, he usually eats on the run. I think it's kind of fun and we can usually find something healthy to eat.

I couldn't wait to see Henry and Grace again. When I lived in New York full-time they were my favorite kids to baby-sit for. They live near the Museum of Natural History and Henry is wild about the dinosaurs. It's fun to go there with them.

Dad came out of his bedroom looking like Mr. Professional in a light gray summer suit. "Ready?" he asked, taking his briefcase from the coffee table.

"I think so," I said. We were at the door when I stopped. "One sec!" I called, hurrying back into the apartment. In my suitcase, I found my Kid-Kit, which I'd packed. "Ready," I told Dad, running out to the hall.

We bought breakfast and ate it in the cab. (I had a corn muffin and a carton of milk.) The morning traffic crawled through the streets. I felt as if we'd never get across town, but finally we did. "Have a good day. See you tonight,"

Dad said, giving me a kiss as I climbed out of the cab. "Say hello to the Walkers for me."

"Okay." As the car pulled away I turned and looked up at the huge apartment building in front of me. In a flash I remembered when I'd lived in this building. It hadn't been a particularly happy time because Mom and Dad were always fighting. In fact, I'd probably cried a zillion tears in this building.

But there had been some good times, too. I was glad to be back for a visit.

I entered the lobby and spoke to the doorman. "Hi," I said, not sure if he remembered me. "I'm here to see the Walkers in eighteen-E."

He smiled and picked up the phone on the wall. "Ms. McGill is here," he said into it. He did remember me! "Go on up."

It was strange being in the lobby, as if I'd gone back in time. I felt as if I'd never left. I half expected to go to the twelfth floor where we used to live, and hear Mom and Dad screaming at each other from down the hall.

"Nice to see you," the doorman said as I headed to the elevator.

"You, too," I called back to him.

On the eighteenth floor I rang the doorbell of apartment E and Mrs. Walker answered. "Stacey!" she cried happily. "Come in!"

"Your hair looks great that way," I said sincerely. She'd cut her curly, medium length black hair very short. Now her cap of short curls set off her large, dark, carefully lined eyes and showed off the dangling bronze earrings she wore. They spun on either ear like tiny mobiles.

"Thanks," she said. "This is a new stage in my career so I figured I needed a new look."

I stepped into the apartment and gazed around at the artwork on the walls. Most of it is modern, which is not really my favorite. Somehow, though, it looked right in the Walkers' place. So did the sculptures and wall hangings that were everywhere. I noticed that they'd acquired a new sculpture since I was there last. It wasn't of anything in particular, just different colors of metal that intertwined in an interesting way. I liked it, which I hoped meant my taste was becoming more sophisticated.

Their apartment was laid out just like our old one, with the rooms in the same arrangement. But it looked very different. For one thing, they had turned the dining room into an artist's studio. There were no curtains or shades on the windows because Mr. Walker, who is a painter, wants the soft, northern light to stream in without any shadows. His easel and chair were near the window on the left side of the room.

Mrs. Walker, who is an illustrator, also wants the benefit of good lighting on her slanted desk by the window on the right side of the room. I noticed a very large pastel drawing on her desk. It seemed to be about three-quarters finished. It showed an African-American woman in an old-fashioned outfit, with a big straw hat, standing in a garden. Many smaller characters tumbled from her hands. "This is great," I said sincerely, moving toward the picture.

"Thanks. It's going to be the cover of a book on African-American folk stories," Mrs. Walker said, standing beside me and studying the drawing. "It's not due to the publisher until next month, but I want to finish it for the show. I got this far while the kids were at camp, but since camp ended I haven't even looked at it."

"I'm here now," I said. "So you can start working on it again. Where are the kids?"

Mrs. Walker laughed. "They're in shy mode, hiding in Henry's room."

"Shy?" I cried. "With me?" The Walker kids *are* shy, but they know me well. I suppose I'd been gone longer than I realized.

At that moment I heard giggles from nearby. The moment I turned, Henry and Grace scrambled down the hallway and darted into

Henry's room. "I hear kids!" I shouted play-fully, hurrying down the hall after them. "I hear kids!" I entered Henry's room and heard more giggles. It wasn't hard to tell where they were hiding. Henry was in the closet and Grace was under the bed. "Hmmmm," I said loudly. "Now where did those kids go?"

More giggles.

"I know, they're hiding in the hamper." I lifted the white straw hamper and looked in-side. "No." I walked around the room some more. "Aha! Behind the curtains!" I tossed aside the green curtains covered with a pattern of small zebras.

From under the bed came a yelp of hilarious laughter. Dropping to my knees, I peered un-der the bed. "I found Grace!" I cried, reaching under the bed. Grace stretched out her small, warm hand and grabbed mine. She let me slide her toward me.

"Stacey! Stacey!" she said, hugging me. So much for shyness. I hugged her back, glad to see her again. She's definitely my favorite three-year-old.

"We have to find Henry," I whispered. "Do you know where he is?"

Grace nodded. "But I can't tell," she whis-pered back.

"I understand," I said as something in the closet bumped. Winking at Grace, I tiptoed to the closet and threw it open. "Got you!" I shouted.

"Aughhhhhh!" Henry scrambled past me, yelling and waving his arms in the air. Then he doubled over with laughter.

"Hey there, Henry. How was camp?" I asked as his laughter died down.

"It was good," he said, smiling. "I was the best drawer in my craft group."

"I was too!" Grace said. "I am a good drawer, too!"

"I believe it," I said. I gazed around at the crayon pictures of dinosaurs that covered the room. "These are excellent." They were, too. Henry had obviously inherited his parents' talent.

Both Henry and Grace like artistic activities, such as drawing, painting, and making things from clay. As you can imagine, they always have plenty of materials around. At camp, Henry had built several dinosaur models from Popsicle sticks, which he proudly showed me. His parents had bought him a whole bag of the sticks, so the kids and I spent the next hour gluing sticks together. I made a box. Henry attempted a pterodactyl, which would have been successful if the wings hadn't kept falling off. Grace's hodgepodge of sticks and glue didn't look like anything much, but hey, maybe it was modern art.

Before noon we wandered out to the kitchen for lunch. "Hi there, Stacey," said Mr. Walker, who entered the kitchen just as we did. He's tall and wore a long, white, paint-covered apron over his jeans and shirt. "How's life in the suburbs?"

"Pretty good," I replied.

"I don't believe you," Mr. Walker said, smiling. He pulled a bottle of club soda from the refrigerator and poured himself a drink. He offered me a glass and I took it. "The suburbs are no place for a city girl like you," he continued, putting the bottle back. "You belong here where things are happening."

"I sometimes think the same thing," I admitted. "But I have good friends in Stoneybrook. I like it there."

"You'll come back," Mr. Walker predicted with a sparkle in his eyes. "I know you, Anastasia. You'll be back." It was funny to hear him call me Anastasia. Almost no one does. Sometimes if I'm in trouble one of my parents calls me that. When Mr. Walker said it, though, it sounded cool and artistic.

"Can we have Fluff, Dad?" Henry asked his father. "Peanut butter and Fluff?"

"All right," he said. "But that stuff's supposed to be for dessert."

"Yea! Fluff!" Grace cheered.

I made sandwiches for the kids. As I spread the gooey marshmallow stuff, the doorbell rang several times. The first two times messengers came to the door with things from the Fitzroy Gallery. The third time I heard a male voice in the hallway. "Come in, Ethan," I heard Mrs. Walker say. "Mr. Walker could really use your help. He wants you to hammer together another frame and stretch the canvas. And when you're done with that, I need you to take some more pieces over to the Fitzroy for me."

I couldn't see Ethan, but he had a nice voice. "Sure thing, Mrs. W," he answered.

Then the phone began to ring. By the fourth ring, I ran to pick it up. "Don't answer," Mrs. Walker said, sticking her head into the kitchen. "We're not answering any calls except from the Fitzroy."

She cocked her head, listening to the voice coming over the answering machine. "This is Arnold from the Fitz — "

Mrs. Walker darted across the kitchen and snapped up the phone. "Hi, Arnold."

As the kids sat at the kitchen table and devoured their sticky sandwiches, the phone kept ringing. Sometimes the Walkers took the calls, sometimes they didn't. A man named Antoine showed up and started talking to Mrs.

Walker about how they were going to arrange the show. Mrs. Walker's illustrations would be in one room, Mr. Walker's paintings in another. Mrs. Walker disagreed and thought they should be mingled together.

They were still discussing this as I cleared up the table and shepherded the kids back to their rooms. I planned to take them on some outings, but it seemed best just to stay home and get reacquainted today. The three of us sat on the floor of Henry's room and played Candy Land for awhile, then Henry wanted to play funny freeze tag.

"Okay," I agreed, putting away the board game. In funny freeze tag, you run around acting goofy — hopping, jumping, walking silly. If you get tagged, you have to freeze in that silly position.

We decided to play in the hall. In minutes, the three of us were laughing breathlessly as we ran up and down the hall looking completely ridiculous. Henry had just tagged me as I walked like a chicken, bobbing my head and flapping my elbows. I was frozen in that position, with my back turned, when I heard a voice behind me. "Can anyone join this game?"

I recognized the voice. Ethan's. Slowly, totally embarrassed, I turned.

Ethan was about fifteen. And gorgeous!

Completely, totally gorgeous! He had deep blue eyes and long, almost black hair. He had high cheekbones, a straight nose and a wide mouth. A tiny gold hoop earring dangled from one ear. He was tall with broad shoulders. A Mexican print shirt was loosely tucked into his faded jeans.

Quickly I twisted out of my chicken pose.

"No fair, you were frozen!" Henry protested.

"I'm Ethan. You're Anastasia?" he said with just a touch of adorable shyness.

"Stacey," I said. "That's what everyone calls me."

He nodded. "I'm waiting for Mrs. W. to wrap up her work for me to bring to the gallery," he explained.

"You work there?" I asked.

"Yeah. I was helping at the gallery during the summer. I quit there last week because school is starting, but then the Walkers hired me to help get ready for the show." He smiled. "I thought I'd have this last week for vacation but I couldn't say no to the Walkers. They're so cool and talented. I'm trying to talk Mr. Walker into giving me art lessons."

"You're an artist?" I asked.

"I'd like to be," he said.

"Hey, what happened to our game?" Henry asked indignantly.

"Sorry, Henry," I apologized.

"I'll be It," Ethan volunteered.

"Okay," Henry agreed.

So Ethan joined the game. He was great with the kids, and came up with some hilarious steps when it was his turn to run. He turned his feet in and walked with his knees knocking, his arms flapping. Like a little kid, he didn't care how silly he looked.

Ethan played with us for about twenty minutes until Mrs. Walker had her artwork ready for him. He was so funny and easy to be around that I stopped feeling nervous near him.

For the rest of the day, every time I heard the bell ring, I peeked to see if it was Ethan, but he didn't come back.

"Does Ethan come by every day?" I asked Mrs. Walker around six-thirty when I was leaving.

"Yes," Mrs. Walker said, smiling. "Are you interested?"

"Oh, no," I replied, blushing. "I have a boyfriend at home. And besides, you know, we just met. We don't even know each other. No. No."

Mrs. Walker kept smiling. She didn't look convinced. "He's so talented. Really gifted. And a nice young man."

"He did seem nice," I said, trying to sound casual.

"Thanks so much, Stacey," Mrs. Walker said as she accompanied me to the front door. "See you tomorrow."

That night, Dad and I ate at the Lion's Lair on 70th Street. It was warm enough so that we could eat in the back on the open patio, which was next to a huge rock ledge. Around us the lights from apartment buildings lit up one by one as the sun set behind the ledge. While we ate, I told Dad about my first day at the Walkers'.

"So, I guess you liked this guy, Ethan," Dad observed with a wry smile.

I stared at him. "Why do you say that?"

"You've mentioned him about six times so far and you've only been there one day."

"Yeah . . . well . . . he was nice," I said, "but it's not what you're thinking."

"What am I thinking?" he asked.

"You know what you're thinking and it's not true," I said adamantly.

"Okay, okay." Dad waved his white cloth napkin like a surrender flag. "Let's order dessert. They've had great fresh berries here lately."

That night, as soon as we got back to the apartment, I phoned Robert.

The line was busy. I called him back every fifteen minutes for the next hour and a half.

But the line stayed busy.

CHAPTER 11

I was having such a great time at the Walkers' that Tuesday and Wednesday just flew by. Both nights I came home exhausted but happy. Dad and I would eat supper, rent a video, and then go to sleep early. At night before going to bed I thought about Robert a lot, wondered what he was doing. I didn't try calling him again, though, because I was too tired even to talk. Still, I wondered why he hadn't called me.

That Wednesday night I had my hand on the phone in the living room, about to try Robert's number, when it rang. "Hello?" I answered, hoping it would be Robert.

"Hi. It's me." It was Claudia. Oh, well. I was glad to hear from her. I settled in on the couch, cradling the phone under my chin, preparing for a good long chat with my best friend.

"How's it going?" she asked.

"Great," I told her enthusiastically. "The Walkers' place is a madhouse of people coming and going, but Grace and Henry are as cute as ever. Yesterday I took them to the Museum of Natural History. We had a ball. You should see the new dinosaur exhibit they have there. It is so cool! Henry and Grace have already seen it a billion times, of course, but Ethan and I hadn't, so we — "

"Ethan?" Claudia interrupted.

"Yes. He's this very, *very* cute guy who is working for the Walkers. He was going down in the elevator with us so we started talking about the museum and he came with us."

"Very cute, huh?" Claudia said, interested.

"Very," I repeated. She asked me a few more questions about him — how tall, how old, what color eyes — and I filled her in. "But it's no big deal," I added. "He's just this really nice guy who is around a lot. You should have seen him when we went skating with the kids in Central Park today."

"Isn't it a little warm for skating?" Claudia asked.

"In-line, silly." I laughed. "Man, can he Rollerblade! He can do spins and jumps and everything. I felt like a snail compared to him. But, you know, he wasn't a show-off at all. He was only doing those tricks because Henry asked him to. He was so good with Henry. So

111

patient. He taught him how to Rollerblade. At first Henry was afraid, but by the end of the afternoon he could do it. Ethan was a big help because Henry felt proud of himself, and I was free to help Grace who is still on training roller skates."

"He sounds great," Claudia commented.

"Oh, he is," I agreed. "What's happening in Stoneybrook?"

"The Mexican festival, mostly," she told me.

"How's that going?"

"Don't ask!"

"Bad?"

"*Mucho* bad. Abby is just moving way too fast on this. Nothing is planned right. She keeps hitting us up for money to pay for her little projects. Out of the blue, she decided we had to give out fliers. I was up until midnight last night drawing sombreros. She's having them copied today and the festival is this Saturday."

"Kristy would laugh if she heard all this," I said.

"She'd laugh or she'd have a fit," Claudia said. "This reminds me of the time we went to California and saw how disorganized the We Love Kids Club was. Remember how that nearly drove Kristy insane?"

I laughed, remembering how out of hand

things can get when events and schedules aren't properly organized.

"This is going to be more of a fiasco than a festival if you ask me," Claudia said.

"Good luck," I told her. "I bet Abby pulls through at the end."

"I sure hope so."

There was a slight pause in our conversation. I was going to tell Claud about my plans to take the Circle Line boat tour around Manhattan the next day, when she started talking.

"Tomorrow, I'm — "

"Stacey, I — " Our voices overlapped and we laughed.

"You go first," I said.

Claudia sighed miserably. "Stacey, I . . . I have some bad news."

I straightened up, sitting forward on the couch. "What?"

"It's about Robert."

My heart slammed into my chest. "Is he all right?" I asked urgently.

"Fine. He's fine," Claudia assured me. Then what could it be? I waited. "I think . . . I mean, I'm pretty sure . . . I'm positive, really . . . Stacey, Robert has been seeing Andi Gentile."

I heard her words . . . but I didn't.

"Stacey?" Claudia spoke into the phone. "Stacey, are you there?"

"Yeah."

"I wouldn't tell you if I wasn't sure," Claudia went on. "But people have been seeing them together all week. Emily Bernstein saw them at Casa Grande again. Mal and Jessi spotted them playing tennis. All the while I kept telling myself it might be nothing but then I saw them myself today. They were downtown and . . . and . . . it's not nothing."

"What do you mean?" I asked quietly. Claudia mumbled something so fast I couldn't hear it. "What?"

She spoke quickly again, but this time I caught the words. "I said he kissed her."

"On the lips?" I hated to ask but I needed to know.

"Yeah."

"You saw it yourself?"

"Yeah. I did."

We were both quiet then, just hanging on the line. "Thanks for telling me," I said finally.

"Are you all right, Stacey?"

"I think so. I'm not sure. It doesn't seem real yet."

"I guess you were right to feel suspicious of him."

I nodded over the phone, which shows you the kind of shape I was in. Dazed, I suppose. Although I'd worried about this, somehow now that my fears were confirmed, I didn't want to even think about it. I guess I really am nonconfrontational. I sure didn't want to face this. "I'm going to hang up now. Okay?" I said.

"Okay. I'll call you tomorrow to make sure you're all right."

"Thanks, Claudia. 'Bye." For a moment, I sat on the couch, just staring. How could this be? For the last several months, since I'd started seeing Robert, part of being me was being Stacey and Robert.

Stacey and Robert 2-gether 4-ever. At least that's what I'd scribbled on my school notebooks. That's what I'd thought. Or, maybe I simply hadn't thought. I'd just assumed we'd keep going along and going along. I hadn't really *thought* about the future, not seriously. Yet I'd expected that Robert would always be there with me. Weren't we close? Didn't we care for and look out for one another? Didn't we enjoy spending time together? Wasn't that the way it was?

How had this happened?

A tear ran down my cheek. Andi couldn't take Robert away from me. She couldn't! I wouldn't let her! Who did she think she was? Robert was *my* boyfriend. Mine.

Now tears gushed from my eyes. I jammed

the palms of my hands into them. I didn't want to cry. But I couldn't help it. The tears kept coming.

I heard Dad's keys in the lock and jumped up from the couch. If he saw me crying he'd want to talk and I couldn't stand to talk about that just then. Blinded by tears I ran to my room.

"Stacey, are you here?" Dad called as he stepped into the apartment.

"In my room!" I shouted back, making my voice as steady as I could.

I could tell from his voice that he was outside my bedroom door. "Samantha and I want to take you out to eat," he said.

"You go," I shouted through the closed door. "I'm pooped."

"Stacey, open up, please." There was no getting out of it. Drying my eyes on the bedsheet, I opened the door. "You've been crying!" Dad gasped. "What happened?"

"Robert is seeing someone else!" I blurted out, tears flooding me once again. Dad put his arms around me and I sobbed into his white work shirt. I cried for several minutes before looking up.

Dad asked if I was sure and I told him what Claudia told me. "Why don't you call Robert yourself?" he suggested.

Call Robert? The idea horrified me. I

couldn't. What would I say? What would he say? "I can't, Dad. I can't," I sobbed.

Dad nodded sympathetically. "Wipe your eyes and then come out to eat with Samantha and me. She's waiting downstairs in a cab."

Samantha, Dad's friend, is pretty nice. I didn't mind going out with her. But I was in the mood to be by myself. I told Dad that, but he insisted. "You shouldn't be alone right now," he said. "Come on."

So I went. Dad and Samantha had planned to go to a burger place, but Dad switched plans. He told the cab driver to take us to Joe Allen's which is one of my favorite restaurants in New York. We had a nice meal, though I probably wasn't much company. I hardly said anything. I'm sure Samantha sensed something was wrong, but she didn't ask.

That night, after I said good night to Dad, I turned out the lights but I couldn't sleep. I lay awake staring at the light the streetlamp threw across my ceiling. What would Robert say if I asked him what was going on? I wondered about it and the more I wondered, the more I had to know.

I got out of bed and went quietly into the living room. There was no real need to turn on the lights because a streetlamp outside the window lit the room well enough for me to see the phone.

It was about nine forty-five. Robert's family didn't go to bed until ten.

I dialed Robert's number. His sister answered. "Is Robert there, please?" I said.

"I'll get him," she said.

I heard her call him. In the distance I could hear him ask her something. "No, I don't know who it is," she shouted back, sounding irritated. I heard his blurred, indistinct voice again. "Yes. It's a girl," his sister shouted. "No, I'm not asking who it is. I'm not your secretary."

"Hello?" Robert said.

I opened my mouth to speak. Only a croaking sound came out. What would I say to him? I hung up.

Clutching the phone in the dark, I hung my head and sobbed.

CHAPTER 12

"Is something the matter?" Ethan asked me the next day as we stood on the top deck of the Circle Line boat. The boat was cruising past the gigantic Twin Towers at the southern tip of Manhattan. Henry leaned on the railing, gazing out at the impressive city skyline. Behind us, Grace had conked out, snoozing peacefully on a bench.

"It's nothing," I replied. "A personal thing." Of course, I was thinking about Robert.

"You seem really bummed," Ethan observed.

I forced a smile. "I didn't know it showed. Sorry."

"That's okay. Can I help?"

I shook my head. "Thanks anyway."

"The opening tomorrow night will cheer you up," he said. "I can't wait."

A breeze off the Hudson River whipped my

hair into my face. Pushing it back, I looked at Ethan. He had such a *nice* face. I was comfortable with him. He was just very thoughtful, and a lot of fun. "Will you be at the opening?" I asked.

"Yeah, and I'm totally psyched. The show is going to be awesome. I can't believe the Walkers pulled it off. Last week they were so far behind. They didn't have nearly enough stuff finished or framed. But with you here this week, they accomplished a lot. You saved the day."

"No, I didn't." I laughed. "I only baby-sat."

"Believe me, it made a big difference," he insisted. "Anyway, wait until you see the show. It's great. A lot of important people will be there to see it."

"Artists?" I asked.

"Artists, and gallery owners, and art critics. Publishing people will be there because Mrs. Walker does book and magazine illustrations. Almost everyone they invited accepted."

"I guess it will be pretty exciting," I said.

"Super exciting. It will even convince you to move back to the city."

I smiled. "You think?"

"I hope," he said seriously.

The tingling sensation at my temples told me I was blushing. Mortified, I turned away. Blushing like that was such a childish thing to do. But despite my embarrassment, I felt happy. I was glad Ethan wished I lived in the city. It made me wish I lived in the city full-time, too.

When the tingling subsided, I turned back to Ethan. "That's nice of you to say," I told him. "I sort of live in the city, really. I'm here a lot of weekends."

"That's true," he said, smiling. We looked at each other and I was aware that my heart was pounding.

Just then, Grace stirred on the bench. Rubbing her eyes, she sat up. "Hi," I said, joining her. "Did you have a good nap?"

She nodded sleepily. Henry sat on the bench with us. "I'm hungry," he said. Grace was, too, so we went inside and bought some snacks. From then on, the kids were awake and curious about everything they saw. Ethan and I pointed out the Empire State Building and other sights as we passed them.

When the tour ended, we took a cab back to the Walkers'. "Hey, want to go see the star show at the planetarium?" Ethan suggested.

"Yea!" Henry cheered.

"Good idea!" I agreed. I wanted to stay busy. I didn't want time to think about Robert. "Don't you have to help hang the rest of the show, though?" I asked Ethan.

"Not until this evening."

"Great," I said. We went to the planetarium and saw the show. Even Grace liked it since she thought it was exciting to sit in a dark theater looking up at stars and planets. After that, we walked back to the Walkers' apartment together.

"How was your day?" Mr. Walker asked the kids as they ran to him and hugged him. He looked frazzled, with a thin smear of hot pink paint across his forehead and a patch of pearly white paint in his hair. He'd been working hard this week.

"It was great," Henry told him, smiling.

"Ethan, I could use you here a minute," Mrs. Walker said. She was fitting one of her paintings with a mat and frame. Ethan joined her. "Hold this steady for me, would you?" Mrs. Walker asked.

It was time for me to go, so I said good-bye and left. On the street, I hailed a cab. As soon as I sat down, I felt terrible. By myself there was no distraction from my thoughts. I kept picturing Andi with Robert. It was awful, but I couldn't stop thinking about it.

What was so special about Andi? Nothing that I could see. How could he like her better than me? Why had he stopped liking me? What had I done wrong? Maybe he needed somebody who didn't baby-sit and who didn't go away every other weekend, someone who was there all the time.

I thought of a million things that might be the matter with me. Every insecurity I'd ever felt came zooming back. Was something wrong with my personality? My looks? Was I too thin? Was it the diabetes? Did he want a girlfriend who could eat ice cream and junk food with him?

Did he want someone who was part of his old crowd? It could be. Maybe I took him away from his old friends too much. He might want a girlfriend who fit in better.

By the time the cab pulled up to my dad's apartment on 65th Street, I felt like screaming. I couldn't stand the thoughts I was thinking. I longed to turn them off, but I couldn't.

Dad wasn't home yet, so I turned on the TV. I watched every rerun that came on, one after the other, without even channel surfing for something good. When I couldn't stand it any longer, I dialed Robert's number again.

Busy.

Was he talking to Andi? Somehow I was positive he was.

Dad came in around seven. He was in a great mood — too great. I could tell he was trying to be super upbeat for my sake. "Come on," he said cheerfully. "We're going to the theater!"

"The theater?" I repeated.

"Yup. We have an intern at work and there's really not much for her to do, so I asked her to go stand on line at the TKTS booth and get us half-price tickets for a Broadway show."

"You shouldn't have made your intern do your personal stuff," I scolded. "That's not right."

Dad pulled off his tie. "She was glad to do it. She wanted the chance to get tickets for herself, too."

"I suppose that's all right then," I said. I was glad about the tickets. If I'd had to sit around the apartment thinking about Robert all night I might have gone nuts.

We went to Joe Allen's again for dinner and then to the theater. The musical we saw was fun and uplifting. Dad was great, too. He didn't mention Robert or ask me how I was feeling. It was just what I needed.

The next day, entering the Walkers' apartment was like walking into a hurricane. People from the gallery carried out paintings and illustrations. The Walkers themselves both worked feverishly, adding last-minute touches to the artwork still in front of them.

Ethan hurried past me carrying one of Mr. Walker's paintings. He smiled and nodded at me, but was too rushed to stop. "Come on, kids," I said, going down the hall to Henry's room. "We're going out."

Grace hopped out into the hall. "Hurray! Hurray!" she cried, bouncing as if her feet had springs.

Henry came out and folded his arms.

"What's wrong?" I asked.

"No one is paying any attention to us," he complained. "This morning, Mommy told me to pour my own cereal."

"You're big enough to do that," I said with a smile.

Henry shook his head. "The Rice Krispies fell on the floor and I spilled the milk."

"Bummer. What did your mom do?"

"She looked up at the ceiling and said, 'Give me strength!' How could the ceiling give her strength?"

"Cereal is not heavy," Grace added.

That made me laugh. "She didn't need strength to pick up the cereal. She just . . ." How could I explain it? "She's just very busy right now. We'll go out so she can get her work done."

I took the kids to the Central Park Zoo. They had a great time, especially watching the seals perform their tricks. We had lunch in the park. They ate hot dogs and I ordered a knish from a vendor. I bought them helium balloons from

125

another vendor and let them run around in the park, trailing their balloons behind them.

It was a fun day. Late that afternoon, when we returned, everything was quiet. We read books and soon Mr. Walker came in, still paint-splattered but looking much calmer.

"You can go home early," he told me. "Get ready for the opening. That's what Mrs. W. is doing right now. We'll bring Henry and Grace to the opening and you can meet us there."

"All right," I said, closing the picture book I was reading to the kids. "Good luck."

I went home and showered. I decided to wear the black dress and a pair of black sandals. I fixed my hair in a French braid and put on a pair of gold hoop earrings. After a quick salad, I cabbed it to the Fitzroy Gallery.

There were actually limousines in front of the gallery when I arrived. I hopped out and went inside. Everything looked great. The paintings were all framed and hanging. Small lights shone across some of them. Mrs. Walker's illustrations and Mr. Walker's paintings were on different walls, but in the same rooms. Jazz music wafted through the gallery. At the far end of the main room people milled in front of a refreshment table. A huge bouquet of tall, orange flowers with pointy petals sat in the middle of the table looking like exotic wild birds.

"Stacey!" Mrs. Walker called me. She looked gorgeous in a flowing gold, purple, and orange African print gown. Her dangling earrings glistened with metallic pieces. (Very artistic. Claudia would have adored them!) Henry and Grace were with her. Henry wore a white shirt and black pants. Grace had on a wonderful party dress of cobalt blue with a lace collar. "You look lovely," Mrs. Walker told me.

"You too!" I said sincerely. "So do you, Henry and Grace." I took their hands and we walked over to the refreshment table. They picked at the wide array of foods. I bit into a fat, fresh strawberry and looked around. I spotted Ethan wearing jeans, a white T-shirt, and a lightweight gray sports jacket. He looked awesome.

In a minute, we made eye contact. He waved and came over. "Pretty cool, huh," he commented.

"Extremely," I agreed.

"You look gorgeous," he said.

"Thank you. You look great, too."

I can't begin to tell you what a wonderful night it was. Henry and Grace were angels. Ethan stayed with me as much as he could. Every once in awhile he had to rush off to help with something, but he came back often. He pointed out all the important artists and art

dealers, museum curators, and gallery owners. He knew everyone — who they were and
what they did. Being there with him as a guide
was so much more interesting than it would
have been otherwise.

Henry and Grace both got sleepy around
eight o'clock. I told Mr. and Mrs. Walker I
would take them home. "It's all right," Mr.
Walker said, "there are two beds set up in the
office here. Put them to sleep and then stay
and enjoy the rest of the show."

I stayed in the office with Grace and Henry
until they fell asleep. Ethan came in and laid
his sports jacket over Henry. I found a small
blanket for Grace. "Come on, I'll give you the
official tour of the show," Ethan offered in a
whisper. "I can tell you everything about each
piece."

"Terrific," I said, tiptoeing out of the office.
Ethan and I returned to the main room, which
was now very crowded. It was amazing how
much Ethan knew about the artwork, and
about art in general.

The evening flew by. And I didn't think
about Robert even once.

CHAPTER 13

Saturday,
Okay, okay... so maybe Kristy isn't altogether wrong. I admit it. I could probably learn to plan things better. It's just that I'm a fast person. I think fast. I move fast. I like things to happen fast. It's the way I am. But after the festival is over it wouldn't kill me to slow down and think things through more. A little more, anyway. I wish I had thought a little more today.

Saturday was my last official day of baby-sitting for the Walkers. They needed me so that they could be at the gallery to greet people who were coming to see the show. (It was going to be there for three weeks.) Grace and Henry were tired so we had a stay-at-home day, just watching videos, drawing pictures, and reading books.

That night, when I returned to Dad's, Abby called me. "I heard about the Robert thing," she said. "I just wanted to see if you wanted to talk or anything."

"Thanks, but I'm okay," I told her. "How did the festival go today?"

"It was pretty wild."

When people arrived around noon, the festival wasn't nearly ready. The booths weren't completely built. The food was still heating in Mary Anne's oven. Mallory and Jessi were still concocting the fruit punch. Everything was half done.

But cars were pulling into Mary Anne's driveway and parking out on Burnt Hill Road. I guess everyone had end-of-summer boredom and parents were dying to find fun things for their kids to do. Our clients were among the first to show up: the Newtons, the Prezziosos, the Papadakises, the Braddocks. Carolyn and

Marilyn Arnold came wearing identical Mexican hats. Charlotte Johanssen wore a Mexican dress her parents had brought back from vacation.

"What do we do?" Abby asked, panicking. "We have to tell them to come back later."

"We can't!" Claudia cried. "That would be terrible."

Claudia, Jessi, and Mary Anne looked at one another. What could they do? "What would Kristy do?" Claudia asked.

"Forget about Kristy," Abby scolded. "You have to make me a sign that says *closed*."

"Kristy would find a way to stall, yet keep everyone happy at the same time," Mary Anne said, frowning as she thought hard about the problem.

"Face painting!" Claudia cried. "I have my face painting sticks. I could do that while everyone finishes getting ready."

"Great!" Mary Anne agreed. "And I'll bring out Dad's tapes of Mexican music and play them on the portable player. It'll make things seem more festive."

As Mr. Spier's tape, *Sounds of Mexico*, came on, Claudia took out her face paints and unfolded her director's chair. "Free face painting!" she cried. "Free face painting. This hour only."

The group flocked around her. They watched her work on each kid. Jessi and Mallory came around with paper cups of their fruit punch and gave them out free.

Meanwhile, Abby flew around putting things together. She strung up *piñatas*, draped crepe paper, tacked signs on booths. Mary Anne and Jessi helped her, but they quickly realized they'd never get it done fast enough.

"Kristy asks associate members to pitch in when we can't do everything ourselves," Mary Anne said to Abby. "I'll call Logan and Shannon to come help us."

Abby wished everyone would stop talking about Kristy. It made her feel as if she weren't in charge at all. She felt as if Kristy were in charge even though she wasn't there.

"Why don't you call Anna?" Mallory suggested to Abby. "She cares about the orphanage, too. She might even be able to round up a few friends from her orchestra group."

Abby really wanted to do this on her own, but she had to admit she needed help. Claudia couldn't paint faces for hours, and that's how long it would take to do everything that had to be done.

Mary Anne ran into the house and phoned Logan. Logan agreed to help and said he'd call Shannon. Then Abby got Anna on the phone. Anna said she'd come right over with Shannon and that she'd try to recruit a few more people she knew.

Mallory came in to get more punch as Abby hung up the phone. "I'll call Ben Hobart," she said. "He might be able to come over and help."

"Good idea," said Abby.

Within the hour, Logan and Ben arrived. Shannon and Anna came right after them. Three friends of Anna's showed up, too. "Just tell us what to do," Shannon said to Abby.

Abby gave everyone a job. Mary Anne kept the music going and Claudia kept painting faces. Logan finished painting signs. Shannon and Anna used hammers and nails to finish putting booths together. Ben helped Mallory and Jessi set up the refreshment table.

When the Pikes arrived, Mallory put the triplets and Vanessa to work. Vanessa was in charge of sitting at the spin-art booth where people would get to make their own swirling paint creations on an electric wheel. The triplets were each in charge of a different game. Byron took the beanbag toss (which Abby was still working on, stitching up little bags filled with dried beans). Jordan manned the ring toss, and Adam was in charge of the water balloon game in which people tried to burst a water balloon on a picture of a distressed, red-faced person overheating from eating a hot chili pepper.

Abby noticed that Claudia was painting the last kid on her line. It was Jamie Newton and she was giving him the tiger face he'd requested. She glanced at Abby with a worried, "what now?" expression, but Abby gave her the thumbs-up signal.

Everything was ready to go.

By then, people were flooding in. Abby could see that — based on the number of people there — they were going to raise a fortune for the orphanage. Kids were already paying a quarter for a chance to bat at the hanging *piñatas* with a long stick. She heard a water balloon splat against the face of the chili-pepper eater. "A winner!" Adam cried, handing the boy one of the colorful Pogs that they'd bought as prizes. (And for which Abby had requested yet more donations in order to afford.)

Abby slumped against a tree and took a deep breath. Everything was going well. This festival was going to be a success. But had *she* made it a success? Or had all the Kristy thinkalikes saved her? It was an unsettling question.

Abby had been confident she could handle things — and handle them her way. She was sure Kristy was a fanatic who overdid everything.

Now she wasn't as sure. Maybe Kristy knew more about running things than Abby had realized. But Abby was willing to learn, although she'd probably never admit it to Kristy.

CHAPTER 14

I woke up early on Sunday morning even though I didn't have to. I opened my eyes and lay in bed on my side, listening to the city sounds — the traffic, sirens, people on the street — and gazed at the morning sunlight streaming into my room. It was my last day in the city before returning to Stoneybrook. I wanted to savor every last minute of it.

Normally, I'd have been looking forward to getting home after a week away. I missed Mom and my friends.

But this time, when I got home, I'd have to deal with Robert.

That was something I did *not* want to face. As long as I was here I could pretend that nothing had happened. Or that something would change. Robert would see that Andi was a boring little twit and break up with her before I even got home.

Propping myself up on my elbows, I thought about that. It *might* happen. It was certainly possible.

And then I was suddenly completely overwhelmed by the most unbelievable thought — a totally startling, completely shocking realization.

The idea of Robert breaking up with Andi didn't make me happy. In fact, the thought disappointed me.

Could it be? Was it possible that deep down — deep, deep, *deep* down — I was glad to be free of Robert?

Oh, sure, at first it had been a terrible shock. No one likes to be lied to by a person she trusts. And no one wants to be cast aside for someone else. It shakes your trust and hurts your pride.

I'd miss Robert like crazy.

But . . . still and all . . .

There was Ethan.

It wasn't as if I was madly in love with Ethan or that I would have broken up with Robert to go out with him. Now, though, I was free to see more of Ethan if I wanted to. I liked that idea. I liked Ethan.

So, if I liked Ethan, I supposed I couldn't blame Robert much if he liked someone else. (I could still blame him for lying to me, though.)

Dad knocked loudly on my door. "Are you up, Stace?"

"Yes!"

"Are you into going to brunch?"

"Definitely! I'll get ready."

"Give me half an hour to shower and change," he called.

I dressed in black skinny pants and a light pink cardigan. (Another of our Bellair buys.) After picking through my perm, I put on some tannish-pink lipstick and a pair of bead earrings. Then I dragged my suitcase out from under the bed and started packing. I packed fast, throwing my clothes in hastily. Somehow, packing slowly and thoughtfully would have given me time to think about going home. Despite my realization, I was still feeling shaky about it.

By the time Dad was ready, so was I. "Where to?" he asked.

"Somewhere by the Museum of Natural History," I replied. "I'd like to say good-bye to Grace and Henry before I go."

"I know just the place," Dad said. We took a cab to a cafe on the corner by the museum and had a great brunch. I ordered eggs benedict. "Dad, I owe you an apology," I said as we ate.

"For what?" he asked, wiping his mouth with a cloth napkin.

"Last Sunday, in the museum . . . I acted like a little brat."

"No, you didn't."

"Yes I did."

"Well, maybe," he said, laughing.

"I just didn't want to hear what you had to say about Robert. But you were right. You were right about everything."

"Ahhh," Dad said, "that's music to a father's ears."

I laughed. "No, really. I think we *are* too young. Maybe both of us were feeling it but we didn't know. It's better if we date different people. I see that now."

Dad nodded and then reached across the table to place his hand on mine. "Are you all right, Stacey?" he asked. "You can know things are for the best in theory but not feel that way in your heart."

Unexpectedly, his words brought a mist of tears to my eyes. I wondered if that was how he felt about his divorce from Mom. It was surely how I felt about the situation with Robert.

Roughly, I brushed at my eyes. "I'll be okay," I assured him.

Dad patted my hand. "That's my girl."

We finished our brunch and Dad requested the check. "Why don't you run up to the Walkers' while I pay? I'll meet you out front in a cab and we'll go to Grand Central."

"Deal," I said, getting up from the table. I hurried out of the cafe and over to the Walkers' place.

"Stacey, hi," Mrs. Walker greeted me at the door. "I'm so glad you stopped by. I bought you a little something to say thanks." She took a package wrapped in blue tissue paper from the front hall drawer.

"Thanks," I said, pulling apart the tissue. It was a gorgeous pair of hammered bronze earrings, small mobiles, like the kind Mrs. Walker wore.

"A jewelry designer friend of mine makes them," Mrs. Walker explained. "I saw you admiring mine. I hope you like them."

"I do," I said sincerely as I put them on, staring into the front hall mirror. I'd never even told Mrs. Walker how much I liked hers. She'd just noticed. I suppose being observant is a quality good artists have. "Are Henry and Grace around?" I asked. "I'd like to say good-bye."

"Henry! Grace!" Mrs. Walker called down the hall.

The kids came running. "Hi, Stacey!" Henry shouted. "Where are we going today?"

"I'm going home, I'm afraid," I said, bending to his level.

"Why are you afraid?" Henry asked seriously.

"Oh," I said. "That's only an expression." (Although, in a way, I *was* afraid.)

Grace hugged me and then Henry reached over her and added his hug. I squeezed them back. I'd really miss them.

As the hug reached the minute mark, Mrs. Walker gently pried the kids off me. "That's enough now," she told them. "Stacey has to go."

" 'Bye," I said, my hand on the doorknob. "It was a great week."

" 'Bye, Stacey," Mrs. Walker said fondly. "Give our regards to your parents."

"I will." I left the Walkers' and headed down the hall, feeling sad. I pressed the down button on the elevator and waited. When the door opened, Ethan was standing there.

"Stacey!" he cried.

"Hi, Ethan," I said, stepping into the elevator with him. "I'm leaving today, so I came up to say good-bye."

He let the elevator door shut and pressed the down button for me. "You're going down again, too," I reminded him, laughing.

"So what? I don't mind taking a ride with you," he replied, his eyes smiling into mine.

"I'll even go to the station with you, if you want."

"My dad is waiting outside in a cab for me," I told him. "You can come, too."

Ethan shook his head. "No thanks. I want to get all decked out when I meet your dear old dad." We both glanced down at his torn jeans. He probably had the right idea. I was happy to hear him say he planned on meeting Dad. "Listen," he said, suddenly seeming shy. "I'd like to see you again. I mean, when you're in town. Is that okay? Would you like to?"

I nodded, feeling very happy. "I would like to, yeah."

"You're not seeing someone else or anything?"

"I was. But that's over now." Saying the words wasn't nearly as awful as I'd expected.

Ethan smiled. "Do you have a phone number?"

Rummaging in my pocketbook, I found a pen and wrote my city number and my Stoneybrook number on the back of my crumpled ticket for the Circle Line cruise. "There," I said, handing it to him. "What's your number?"

Ethan wrote his number on an old museum ticket I found in my wallet.

He walked me to the front of the building. There weren't any mushy good-byes because

Dad was there in a cab waiting in the street. "I'll call you," Ethan said, waving as I climbed into the cab.

" 'Bye!" I called. And then the cab pulled away. I waved to Ethan until we turned the corner. Then he was gone.

Sitting forward in the seat I thought about going home, and what my next conversation with Robert would be like.

CHAPTER 15

I couldn't believe it. Before I was even at my front door, who came up the street but Andi Gentile. I saw her as Mom and I pulled into the driveway. Couldn't she even wait for me to get my suitcase unpacked before coming over to tell me she'd stolen Robert?

"Is this a friend of yours?" Mom asked, getting out of the car.

"Not exactly," I said as Andi turned up our front walkway. "But I know her."

Mom went into the house and left me standing by the car. Andi stopped and faced me. Her expression was so tortured and unhappy it actually made me feel sorry for her. I didn't want to feel that. I wanted to be angry.

I couldn't help it, though. She looked as if she were about to cry.

"Stacey, I have to tell you something," she began unhappily. "Can we go somewhere and talk?"

"I already know," I said.

"You do?" She gasped. "How . . . could you?"

"Manhattan isn't another planet, you know," I said bitingly. "There are phones there."

"I'm sorry. I didn't mean for it to happen. Robert and I just kept running into each other and when we did we always had a lot to talk about and a lot of laughs and — "

"It's all right," I said, cutting her off. I really didn't want to hear about their good times.

"It's all right?" Andi repeated, daring to step across the lawn toward me. "I don't understand."

"I don't own Robert," I said, and saying the words helped me realize they were true. "If you and Robert want to be together then I can't stop you. I shouldn't stop you."

"I don't want you to hate me, Stacey," said Andi.

"I don't hate you." Oddly enough, that was true, too. I didn't. How could I blame her for liking Robert? I knew how much there was to like about him. "I don't hate you," I repeated more softly. "But I would kind of like to be alone now. Okay?"

"Okay, sure. I'm glad we talked."

"Yeah, me too," I replied, turning toward my house.

Inside, I leaned against the door, catching my breath. Almost immediately, I heard the phone ring. "Yes, she's here, Robert. Just a moment," I heard Mom say into the cordless phone in the dining room. She brought the phone to me. "For you."

"Hi, Stacey," he said. The sound of his voice made my hands shake. "How was the city?"

"Fine," I said, my voice actually trembling.

"Can I come over?" he asked.

"Sure."

"I'm at a phone booth. I'll be there in five minutes."

"Okay." I clicked off and clutched the phone.

"You all right?" Mom asked, seeing my expression.

"Robert and I are about to break up," I told her. "He's coming over now."

Mom bit her lip. "Want me to stay or go?"

"I think we need some privacy," I said.

"All right, but I'll be right upstairs if you need me," she offered, heading up the steps.

"Thanks."

In less than five minutes, Robert showed up. "Hi," he said, looking terribly guilty.

"Come on in," I said, leading the way into the living room. "Before you say anything, Robert," I began, sitting on the couch, "I know what's been happening. Claudia told me and I've already talked to Andi."

Even though the situation was serious, I had to laugh grimly to myself. Robert looked as if he were about to fall off his chair. Eyes wide, he paled and clutched the seat of the chair. "You know?"

I nodded. "What I don't know is why you lied to me." When I said the word *lied* it caught in my throat and came out in a choked way.

"I didn't want to," Robert said, the color returning to his face. In fact, the color was going from white to bright red. "Really, I didn't. I just wasn't sure what was happening and I didn't want to upset you."

"Well, you did upset me!" Now my voice was half sob, half anger.

"I know and I'm sorry. I didn't want to say anything until I *was* sure."

I started crying. "And now you're sure?"

Robert came across the room to the couch. "Why?" I asked through my tears. "Why do you like her better than me?"

Robert took my hand and squeezed it. "I can't explain," he said quietly. "I'm just more relaxed with Andi. I think we have more in common."

"That makes sense, I guess," I said, sniffling.

"I don't have a handkerchief or anything like in the movies," Robert said helplessly. He raised his arm. "Want my sleeve?"

I pushed his arm away, but the offer made me laugh through my tears. "How will I ever find another guy who will let me blow my nose on his sleeve?" Then I started crying again, this time harder than before. The tears gushed out of my eyes like a river overflowing.

"You'll find someone great, Stacey," Robert said tenderly. "Because you're great. You really are. I hope we'll always be friends."

I dried my eyes. "I hope so, too," I said. "Maybe we can be. After awhile." He hugged me hard and I hugged him back.

Then he got up and I could see he wanted to leave. I walked to the door with him. "I'll see you," he said, stepping outside.

"Yeah. See you." I watched him walk away. He turned back once and waved. I waved back, then shut the door.

"How are you?" Mom asked from the stairs behind me.

"I'll live," I said, forcing a smile.

"That's the truth. You will," Mom agreed. "And life is long, you know. You and Robert might get together again. If you were truly meant to be together you will. Look at Mary Anne's father and Dawn's mother."

"I can't think about that," I said. "Right now

it doesn't seem too likely." The phone rang again and I answered it. "Hello?"

"Hi, it's Claud. Are you okay? You sound weird." I told her what had just happened. "Oh, wow," she said. "I'm coming right over."

"You don't have to," I said.

"Yes, I do. I'm your best friend, aren't I?"

"Of course."

"Then I have to come right over."

"All right," I agreed, a smile forming on my face.

"I have the money from the festival to give you, too."

"Why to me?"

"You're the treasurer. Abby said to give it to you. She's glad you're back to take over. I'm not sure she's glad Kristy will be president again, though. It's hard to tell. I think she was getting into the job, but maybe a little too much."

Claudia rambled on about the BSC and everyone we knew. By the time she hung up, I was feeling a lot better. I was glad she was coming over.

As I headed up to my room, I realized it felt good to be home. My future might not include Robert anymore, but I was eager to return to my regular life, see my friends, baby-sit for some of our regular clients.

I'd heard an expression once: sadder but wiser. I hadn't understood it at the time. Now I did. That was me — sadder but wiser Stacey McGill.

I was going to be okay, though. No matter what happened, I'd always have myself to rely on. As long as I liked me, I'd be fine. And that was something I hadn't been sure of before Robert broke my heart. Now I was sure.

Dear Reader,

In *Stacey's Broken Heart*, Stacey is sad about ending her relationship with Robert, but she knows it's for the best, that she has made the right decision. While it wasn't easy for me to write about Stacey's breakup, I always love to write about New York City. I've lived in New York at least part-time since 1979, and when I was a kid, my family lived close enough to the city so that we could visit often.

Many of the places I mention when I write about New York are real. For instance, Stacey's father now lives on East 65th Street. Years ago I lived there, too, with my cat Mouse. Most of the stores are real, such as Bloomingdale's and F.A.O. Schwarz. Many of the restaurants are real, too — The Hard Rock Cafe, Tavern on the Green, Sign of the Dove, and the Oyster Bar. I'm glad Stacey still visits New York from time to time, because then I get to write about it. I hope you like reading about New York. Maybe you'll get to visit sometime!

Happy reading,

Ann M Martin

L. GODWIN

Ann M. Martin

About the Author

ANN MATTHEWS MARTIN was born on August 12, 1955. She grew up in Princeton, NJ, with her parents and her younger sister, Jane.

Although Ann used to be a teacher and then an editor of children's books, she's now a full-time writer. She gets the ideas for her books from many different places. Some are based on personal experiences. Others are based on childhood memories and feelings. Many are written about contemporary problems or events.

All of Ann's characters, even the members of the Baby-sitters Club, are made up. (So is Stoneybrook.) But many of her characters are based on real people. Sometimes Ann names her characters after people she knows, other times she chooses names she likes.

In addition to the Baby-sitters Club books, Ann Martin has written many other books for children. Her favorite is *Ten Kids, No Pets* because she loves big families and she loves animals. Her favorite Baby-sitters Club book is *Kristy's Big Day*. (By the way, Kristy is her favorite baby-sitter!)

Ann M. Martin now lives in New York with her cats, Gussie and Woody. Her hobbies are reading, sewing, and needlework — especially making clothes for children.

Notebook Pages

This Baby-sitters Club book belongs to _____ .

I am _____ years old and in the _____

grade.

The name of my school is _____ .

I got this BSC book from _____ .

I started reading it on _____ and

finished reading it on _____ .

The place where I read most of this book is _____ .

My favorite part was when _____ .

If I could change anything in the story, it might be the part when

_____ .

My favorite character in the Baby-sitters Club is _____ .

The BSC member I am most like is _____

because _____ .

If I could write a Baby-sitters Club book it would be about ___

_____ .

#99 Stacey's Broken Heart

When Stacey finds out that Robert has been seeing another girl, her heart is broken. One person who has broken my heart is

_____ . He/she

broken my heart when _____

_____

_____ . Once I broke someone else's heart by _____

_____

_____ . According to Stacey's father, thirteen is a little young to have a serious relationship. I think a person should be _____ years old before she/he has a serious boyfriend/girlfriend. The most "serious" boyfriend/girlfriend I've had so far is _____ . If I could ask anyone to be my boyfriend/girlfriend, I would ask _____

because _____

_____ .

STACEY'S

Here I am, age three.

Me with Charlot
my "almost

A family portrait — me
with my parents.

SCRAPBOOK

ohanssen,
bister."

Getting ready for school.

In LUV at Shadow Lake.

Illustrations by Angelo Tillery

Read all the books
about **Stacey**
in the Baby-sitters Club series
by Ann M. Martin

3 *The Truth About Stacey*
Stacey's different . . . and it's harder on her than anyone knows.

8 *Boy-Crazy Stacey*
Who needs baby-sitting when there are boys around!

#13 *Good-bye Stacey, Good-bye*
How do you say good-bye to your very best friend?

#18 *Stacey's Mistake*
Stacey has never been so wrong in her life!

#28 *Welcome Back, Stacey!*
Stacey's moving again . . . back to Stoneybrook!

#35 *Stacey and the Mystery of Stoneybrook*
Stacey discovers a *haunted house* in Stoneybrook!

#43 *Stacey's Emergency*
The Baby-sitters are so worried. Something's wrong with Stacey.

#51 *Stacey's Ex-Best Friend*
Is Stacey's old friend Laine super mature or just a super snob?

#58 *Stacey's Choice*
Stacey's parents are both depending on her. But how can she choose between them . . . again?

#65 *Stacey's Big Crush*
Stacey's in LUV . . . with her twenty-two-year-old teacher!

#70 *Stacey and the Cheerleaders*
Stacey becomes part of the "in" crowd when she tries out for the cheerleading team.

#76 *Stacey's Lie*
When Stacey tells one lie it turns to another, then another, then another . . .

#83 *Stacey vs. the BSC*
Is Stacey outgrowing the BSC?

#87 *Stacey and the Bad Girls*
With friends like these, who needs enemies?

#94 *Stacey McGill, Super Sitter*
It's a bird . . . it's a plane . . . it's a super sitter!

#99 *Stacey's Broken Heart*
Who will pick up the pieces?

Mysteries:

1 *Stacey and the Missing Ring*
Stacey has to find that ring — or business is over for the Baby-sitters Club!

#10 *Stacey and the Mystery Money*
Who would give Stacey counterfeit money?

#14 *Stacey and the Mystery at the Mall*
Shoplifting, burglaries — mysterious things are going on at the Washington Mall!

#18 *Stacey and the Mystery at the Empty House*
Stacey enjoys house-sitting for the Johanssens — until she thinks someone's hiding out in the house.

#22 *Stacey and the Haunted Masquerade*
This is one dance that Stacey will *never* forget!

Portrait Collection:

Stacey's Book
An autobiography of the BSC's big city girl.

Look for #100

KRISTY'S WORST IDEA

"Uh, excuse me, Kristy," Claudia said, "we know you're mad at yourself for messing up at the Rodowskys', but don't take it out on us."

"This has nothing to do with the Rodowskys!" I shouted. "This has to do with all of you. What are we here for, guys? To sit around, do homework, and talk about all our great activities?"

"Souds like fud to be," Abby said.

"Lots of *fud*, Abby," I said. "So who needs meeting times and rules and stuff? Why not just hang out any old time? And skip the sitting part. That just gets in the way of the *fud*. I mean, no one has time to sit anymore. I might as well split off by myself. I'll be Kristy's Sitting Service. That's what we're turning into, anyway."

All eyes were on me. Wide and stunned.

"Whoa, easy, Kristy," Logan said.

"Kristy, I don't believe you," Mary Anne whispered. "That was mean."

"Look," I said evenly, "I don't mean to be a jerk. I know this is supposed to be a club. And a club is supposed to be fun. But we're a service, too. A service that relies on happy, steady clients. To keep them, we have to hold up our end of the bargain. And that means sticking to meeting times, being there when they call, and showing good attitude, all the time. If I'm the only one with an open enough schedule — me, Kristy the incompetent, specializing in injured kids — then what's the point? We might as well disband the club. The end. 'Bye-'bye."

"Kristy, aren't you going overboard?" Shannon said.

"Maybe you need to lie down," Claudia suggested.

You know what? I didn't need to lie down. And I wasn't going overboard.

How well do YOU know your BSC trivia?

THE BABY-SITTERS CLUB®

Summer Sweeps

HEY FANS! *BSC Book #100 is coming soon—* can you believe it?—and we're celebrating its arrival with an awesome trivia sweepstakes all summer long!

✱✱✱✱✱✱✱

Enter now to win a part in a future BSC book *plus* more than 100 other sweepstakes prizes!

Enter To Win 100+ Prizes

GRAND PRIZE:
- ✱ You will be featured in a future BSC story
- ✱ A complete wardrobe from LA Gear including an extralarge duffle bag, sweatshirt, t-shirt, baseball cap, shoes, water bottle, and leather CD carrying case
- ✱ *The BSC The Movie* video
- ✱ *The BSC The Movie* sound track
- ✱ BSC t-Shirt
- ✱ *The Complete Guide to The BSC*—autographed by Ann M. Martin

10 FIRST PRIZES:
- ✱ BSC t-Shirt
- ✱ *The Complete Guide to The BSC*—autographed by Ann M. Martin

100 RUNNERS-UP:
- ✱ BSC t-Shirt

It's easy! Just answer the ten questions on the back of this sheet, fill-in your name and address, and send back to us!

MORE ➡

BSCSC296

How well do YOU know your BSC trivia?

THE BABY-SITTERS CLUB®

Summer Sweeps

Enter To Win 100+ Prizes

The Questions:

1. The BSC meets on these days: Monday, Wednesday, and Friday.
2. What day of the week is dues day? Monday.
3. What is the name of the box (with games) that Kristy invented for charges? Kid-Kit.
4. BSC meetings begin at: Claudia
5. Whose bedroom are BSC meetings held in? ______ ______.
6. Which member sits in the director's chair at club meetings? ______ ______.
7. Who is originally from New York City? ______ ______.
8. How many brothers and sisters does Mallory have? ______.
9. Which two members are only eleven years old? ______ and ______.
10. Friends. Members of the BSC. What else do Mary Anne and Dawn have in common? ______.

Just try to answer the questions above and fill out the coupon below, or write the questions and as many answers as you can on a piece of paper and mail to: The BSC Summer Sweeps, Scholastic Inc., P.O. Box 7500, 2931 East McCarty Street, Jefferson City, MO 65102 (Remember to include your name, address, and phone number on your entry). Entries must be postmarked by October 31, 1996. No purchase necessary. Complete/Correct answers not required to win. Enter as often as you wish, one entry to an envelope. Mechanically reproduced entries are void. Scholastic is not responsible for lateness, lost entries, or postage due to mail. Contest open to residents of the U.S.A. and Canada, ages 6 to 15 upon entering. Employees of Scholastic Inc., its agencies, affiliates, subsidiaries, and their families are ineligible. Winners will be selected at random from all official entries received. Winners will be notified by mail. Winners will be required to execute an eligibility affidavit to release the use of their names for any promotional purposes determined by Scholastic Inc. Winners are responsible for all taxes that may be attached to any prize winnings. Prizes may be substituted by Scholastic Inc. For a complete list of winners, send a self-addressed stamped envelope after November 30, 1996 to: The BSC Summer Sweeps Winner List at the address above.

Enter me in The BSC Summer Sweeps!

I am including the answers to the 10 questions.

Name______________________ Birthdate__ __ __
First Last m / d / y

Street______________________

City______________ State______ Zip Code______

(check boxes section please)

Tell Us Where You Got This Book!

__ Bookstore __ Book Club __ Book Fair

__ Price Club __ Other ______

THE BABY-SITTERS CLUB®

The best friends you'll ever have!

Collect 'em all!

by Ann M. Martin

❏ MG43388-1	#1	Kristy's Great Idea	$3.50
❏ MG43387-3	#10	Logan Likes Mary Anne!	$3.99
❏ MG43717-8	#15	Little Miss Stoneybrook...and Dawn	$3.50
❏ MG43722-4	#20	Kristy and the Walking Disaster	$3.50
❏ MG43347-4	#25	Mary Anne and the Search for Tigger	$3.50
❏ MG42498-X	#30	Mary Anne and the Great Romance	$3.50
❏ MG42508-0	#35	Stacey and the Mystery of Stoneybrook	$3.50
❏ MG44082-9	#40	Claudia and the Middle School Mystery	$3.25
❏ MG43574-4	#45	Kristy and the Baby Parade	$3.50
❏ MG44969-9	#50	Dawn's Big Date	$3.50
❏ MG44968-0	#51	Stacey's Ex-Best Friend	$3.50
❏ MG44966-4	#52	Mary Anne + 2 Many Babies	$3.50
❏ MG44967-2	#53	Kristy for President	$3.25
❏ MG44965-6	#54	Mallory and the Dream Horse	$3.25
❏ MG44964-8	#55	Jessi's Gold Medal	$3.25
❏ MG45657-1	#56	Keep Out, Claudia!	$3.50
❏ MG45658-X	#57	Dawn Saves the Planet	$3.50
❏ MG45659-8	#58	Stacey's Choice	$3.50
❏ MG45660-1	#59	Mallory Hates Boys (and Gym)	$3.50
❏ MG45662-8	#60	Mary Anne's Makeover	$3.50
❏ MG45663-6	#61	Jessi and the Awful Secret	$3.50
❏ MG45664-4	#62	Kristy and the Worst Kid Ever	$3.50
❏ MG45665-2	#63	Claudia's Special Friend	$3.50
❏ MG45666-0	#64	Dawn's Family Feud	$3.50
❏ MG45667-9	#65	Stacey's Big Crush	$3.50
❏ MG47004-3	#66	Maid Mary Anne	$3.50
❏ MG47005-1	#67	Dawn's Big Move	$3.50
❏ MG47006-X	#68	Jessi and the Bad Baby-sitter	$3.50
❏ MG47007-8	#69	Get Well Soon, Mallory!	$3.50
❏ MG47008-6	#70	Stacey and the Cheerleaders	$3.50
❏ MG47009-4	#71	Claudia and the Perfect Boy	$3.50
❏ MG47010-8	#72	Dawn and the We Love Kids Club	$3.50
❏ MG47011-6	#73	Mary Anne and Miss Priss	$3.50
❏ MG47012-4	#74	Kristy and the Copycat	$3.50
❏ MG47013-2	#75	Jessi's Horrible Prank	$3.50
❏ MG47014-0	#76	Stacey's Lie	$3.50
❏ MG48221-1	#77	Dawn and Whitney, Friends Forever	$3.50
❏ MG48222-X	#78	Claudia and Crazy Peaches	$3.50

More titles... ▶

The Baby-sitters Club titles continued...

❑ MG48223-8	#79	**Mary Anne Breaks the Rules**	$3.50
❑ MG48224-6	#80	**Mallory Pike, #1 Fan**	$3.50
❑ MG48225-4	#81	**Kristy and Mr. Mom**	$3.50
❑ MG48226-2	#82	**Jessi and the Troublemaker**	$3.50
❑ MG48235-1	#83	**Stacey vs. the BSC**	$3.50
❑ MG48228-9	#84	**Dawn and the School Spirit War**	$3.50
❑ MG48236-X	#85	**Claudi Kishli, Live from WSTO**	$3.50
❑ MG48227-0	#86	**Mary Anne and Camp BSC**	$3.50
❑ MG48237-8	#87	**Stacey and the Bad Girls**	$3.50
❑ MG22872-2	#88	**Farewell, Dawn**	$3.50
❑ MG22873-0	#89	**Kristy and the Dirty Diapers**	$3.50
❑ MG22874-9	#90	**Welcome to the BSC, Abby**	$3.50
❑ MG22875-1	#91	**Claudia and the First Thanksgiving**	$3.50
❑ MG22876-5	#92	**Mallory's Christmas Wish**	$3.50
❑ MG22877-3	#93	**Mary Anne and the Memory Garden**	$3.99
❑ MG22878-1	#94	**Stacey McGill, Super Sitter**	$3.99
❑ MG22879-X	#95	**Kristy + Bart = ?**	$3.99
❑ MG22880-3	#96	**Abby's Lucky Thirteen**	$3.99
❑ MG22881-1	#97	**Claudia and the World's Cutest Baby**	$3.99
❑ MG22882-X	#98	**Dawn and Too Many Baby-sitters**	$3.99
❑ MG69205-4	#99	**Stacey's Broken Heart**	$3.99
❑ MG45575-3		**Logan's Story Special Edition Readers' Request**	$3.25
❑ MG47118-X		**Logan Bruno, Boy Baby-sitter**	
		Special Edition Readers' Request	$3.50
❑ MG47756-0		**Shannon's Story Special Edition**	$3.50
❑ MG47686-6		**The Baby-sitters Club Guide to Baby-sitting**	$3.25
❑ MG47314-X		**The Baby-sitters Club Trivia and Puzzle Fun Book**	$2.50
❑ MG48400-1		**BSC Portrait Collection: Claudia's Book**	$3.50
❑ MG22864-1		**BSC Portrait Collection: Dawn's Book**	$3.50
❑ MG22865-X		**BSC Portrait Collection: Mary Anne's Book**	$3.99
❑ MG48399-4		**BSC Portrait Collection: Stacey's Book**	$3.50
❑ MG47151-1		**The Baby-sitters Club Chain Letter**	$14.95
❑ MG48295-5		**The Baby-sitters Club Secret Santa**	$14.95
❑ MG45074-3		**The Baby-sitters Club Notebook**	$2.50
❑ MG44783-1		**The Baby-sitters Club Postcard Book**	$4.95

Available wherever you buy books...or use this order form.
Scholastic Inc., P.O. Box 7502, 2931 E. McCarty Street, Jefferson City, MO 65102

Please send me the books I have checked above. I am enclosing $_____
(please add $2.00 to cover shipping and handling). Send check or money order—
no cash or C.O.D.s please.

Name_____ Birthdate_____

Address _____

City_____ State/Zip_____

Please allow four to six weeks for delivery. Offer good in the U.S. only. Sorry, mail orders are not available to residents of Canada. Prices subject to change.

BSC296

THE BABY-SITTERS CLUB®

by Ann M. Martin

Collect and read these exciting BSC Super Specials, Mysteries, and Super Mysteries along with your favorite Baby-sitters Club books!

BSC Super Specials

❑ BBK44240-6	Baby-sitters on Board! Super Special #1	$3.95
❑ BBK44239-2	Baby-sitters' Summer Vacation Super Special #2	$3.95
❑ BBK43973-1	Baby-sitters' Winter Vacation Super Special #3	$3.95
❑ BBK42493-9	Baby-sitters' Island Adventure Super Special #4	$3.95
❑ BBK43575-2	California Girls! Super Special #5	$3.95
❑ BBK43576-0	New York, New York! Super Special #6	$3.95
❑ BBK44963-X	Snowbound! Super Special #7	$3.95
❑ BBK44962-X	Baby-sitters at Shadow Lake Super Special #8	$3.95
❑ BBK45661-X	Starring The Baby-sitters Club! Super Special #9	$3.95
❑ BBK45674-1	Sea City, Here We Come! Super Special #10	$3.95
❑ BBK47015-9	The Baby-sitters Remember Super Special #11	$3.95
❑ BBK48308-0	Here Come the Bridesmaids! Super Special #12	$3.95

BSC Mysteries

❑ BAI44084-5	#1	Stacey and the Missing Ring	$3.50
❑ BAI44085-3	#2	Beware Dawn!	$3.50
❑ BAI44799-8	#3	Mallory and the Ghost Cat	$3.50
❑ BAI44800-5	#4	Kristy and the Missing Child	$3.50
❑ BAI44801-3	#5	Mary Anne and the Secret in the Attic	$3.50
❑ BAI44961-3	#6	The Mystery at Claudia's House	$3.50
❑ BAI44960-5	#7	Dawn and the Disappearing Dogs	$3.50
❑ BAI44959-1	#8	Jessi and the Jewel Thieves	$3.50
❑ BAI44958-3	#9	Kristy and the Haunted Mansion	$3.50

More titles ➡

The Baby-sitters Club books continued...

❑ BAI45696-2	#10 Stacey and the Mystery Money	$3.50
❑ BAI47049-3	#11 Claudia and the Mystery at the Museum	$3.50
❑ BAI47050-7	#12 Dawn and the Surfer Ghost	$3.50
❑ BAI47051-5	#13 Mary Anne and the Library Mystery	$3.50
❑ BAI47052-3	#14 Stacey and the Mystery at the Mall	$3.50
❑ BAI47053-1	#15 Kristy and the Vampires	$3.50
❑ BAI47054-X	#16 Claudia and the Clue in the Photograph	$3.50
❑ BAI48232-7	#17 Dawn and the Halloween Mystery	$3.50
❑ BAI48233-5	#18 Stacey and the Mystery at the Empty House	$3.50
❑ BAI48234-3	#19 Kristy and the Missing Fortune	$3.50
❑ BAI48309-9	#20 Mary Anne and the Zoo Mystery	$3.50
❑ BAI48310-2	#21 Claudia and the Recipe for Danger	$3.50
❑ BAI22866-8	#22 Stacey and the Haunted Masquerade	$3.50
❑ BAI22867-6	#23 Abby and the Secret Society	$3.99
❑ BAI22868-4	#24 Mary Anne and the Silent Witness	$3.99
❑ BAI22869-2	#25 Kristy and the Middle School Vandal	$3.99

BSC Super Mysteries

❑ BAI48311-0	The Baby-sitters' Haunted House Super Mystery #1	$3.99
❑ BAI22871-4	Baby-sitters Beware Super Mystery #2	$3.99

Available wherever you buy books...or use this order form.

Scholastic Inc., P.O. Box 7502, 2931 East McCarty Street, Jefferson City, MO 65102-7502

Please send me the books I have checked above. I am enclosing $ _____ (please add $2.00 to cover shipping and handling). Send check or money order — no cash or C.O.D.s please.

Name_____Birthdate_____

Address _____

City_____State/Zip_____

Please allow four to six weeks for delivery. Offer good in the U.S. only. Sorry, mail orders are not available to residents of Canada. Prices subject to change.

BSCM296

THE BABY-SITTERS CLUB®

by Ann M. Martin

Meet the best friends you'll ever have!

Collect Them All!

Have you heard? The BSC has a new look — and more great stuff than ever before. An all-new scrapbook for each book's narrator! A letter from Ann M. Martin! Fill-in pages to personalize your copy! Order today!

☐ BBD22473-5	#1	Kristy's Great Idea	$3.50
☐ BBD22763-7	#2	Claudia and the Phantom Phone Calls	$3.99
☐ BBD25158-9	#3	The Truth About Stacey	$3.99
☐ BBD25159-7	#4	Mary Anne Saves the Day	$3.50
☐ BBD25160-0	#5	Dawn and the Impossible Three	$3.50
☐ BBD25161-9	#6	Kristy's Big Day	$3.50
☐ BBD25162-7	#7	Claudia and Mean Janine	$3.50
☐ BBD25163-5	#8	Boy-Crazy Stacey	$3.50
☐ BBD25164-3	#9	The Ghost at Dawn's House	$3.99
☐ BBD25165-1	#10	Logan Likes Mary Anne!	$3.99
☐ BBD25166-X	#11	Kristy and the Snobs	$3.99
☐ BBD25167-8	#12	Claudia and the New Girl	$3.99
☐ BBD25168-6	#13	Good-bye Stacey, Good-bye	$3.99
☐ BBD25169-4	#14	Hello, Mallory	$3.99
☐ BBD25170-8	#15	Little Miss Stoneybrook ... and Dawn	$3.99
☐ BBD60410-4	#16	Jessi's Secret Language	$3.99

Available wherever you buy books, or use this order form.

SCHOLASTIC

BSCE296

THE BABY-SITTERS CLUB®

Get ready for the 100th BSC book!

Kristy's Worst Idea
The Baby-sitters Club #100
by Ann M. Martin

It seems like just yesterday Kristy had her great idea to start a club for baby-sitters. Since then, The BSC has gone through some changes. There have been lots of laughs, friendships, and special memories along the way. But now in the 100th Baby-sitters Club book, things happen to make Kristy rethink her great idea...and disband The BSC! Could this really be the end of The Baby-sitters Club?

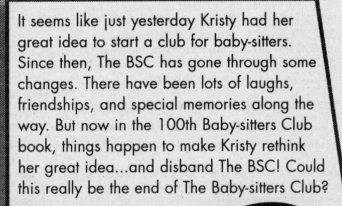

Comes with a special gift for you!

It's the book that no BSC fan should miss— coming soon to a bookstore near you!

■ SCHOLASTIC

BSCT296